# THE DRAGON'S EGG
## and other stories

Born in Warwickshire, England, W. J. Corbett
joined the Merchant Navy as a galley-boy when he
was sixteen and saw the world. Later, during National
Service, he became an Army Physical Training
Instructor. Now living in Birmingham, the author has
also worked as a factory hand, furniture mover,
building-site labourer and dishwasher. His first book,
*The Song of Pentecost*, won the prestigious
Whitbread Award.

"Mr Corbett has wit, originality and economy with
words which put him straight in the very top class
of all . . . beside the authors of such classics as
*The Wind in the Willows, The Jungle Book*
and *B . . .*

Auberon W

# THE
# DRAGON'S EGG
## and other stories

W. J. Corbett

Illustrated by Wayne Anderson

Hodder
Children's
Books

a division of Hodder Headline plc

Printed and bound in Great Britain by
Mackays, Chatham, Kent

Hodder Children's Books
A Division of Hodder Headline plc
338 Euston Road
London NW1 3BH

# CONTENTS

*To four sisters,*
*Rita and Nan,*
*Dora and Dos.*

# SNIFFY
## COMES IN FROM THE COLD

⌐◝

G eorge found his new friend in the
woods at the bottom of the garden. He
was kicking through the autumn leaves
when he uncovered a large pair of nostrils.
Burrowing deeper he discovered a large dragon,
blinking, as if emerging from a very deep sleep.

"I'm George," said the boy.

"And I'm Sniffy," said the dragon, sneezing.

"You certainly are," said George. "You have a
very bad cold there."

"The story of my life," said the dragon, sadly. "I've had millions of colds and bouts of 'flu in my time."

"Which would leave you very little time to be fierce," said George. "I mean, you haven't even breathed fire at me yet. So, shall we be friends?"

"Only if our friendship remains a secret," said the dragon, sniffing nervously. "If St George found out I was still around I'd be in deep trouble. He'd come charging into these woods with his lance at the ready threatening all kind of nasty things."

"Then a secret our friendship shall be," replied the boy.

Though George was very sad about that. His dream was to take his friend to school and see the envy in every one's eyes. For who else could claim that their best friend was a blue dragon with orange spots and easily twenty five feet long? But Sniffy refused to meet the public, preferring to stay hidden away in the woods. George would visit his friend as often as possible, always bringing a few bitter green lemons which seemed to ease Sniffy's constant colds. Sniffy explained that he would like to have been a dangerous dragon but his health had always been too delicate. Born hundreds of years ago with a very bad cold on his chest his fire-breathing had never amounted to more than a few damp puffs and smoke and sparks.

"I'll bet you wish you were like the dragons in my book," George sympathised. "One cousin of yours could scorch off a peacock's tail at fifty feet. But don't worry, Sniffy, I'll never betray you if St George comes thundering through the woods. Though I must say I don't think St George is alive anymore. He appears only in history books these days."

"So what was that clanking sound I heard the other day?" asked Sniffy, sneezing violently. "I distinctly heard the sound of shining armour rattling around the edge of the woods."

"Don't be silly, that was the dustmen emptying their bins," chided George. "My, but in all the dragon books, you are made of braver stuff than that. So what happened between you and St George all those centuries ago? You promised to tell me for my exercise book. And please don't make me mark you down as a coward."

"Well the maiden was tied to the stake as arranged and then St George came galloping down, his lance aimed at my heart," remembered Sniffy, mournfully. "I took the job because it paid treble wages, and my family needed the money. I was meant to die you see."

"But surely you were determined to die bravely," cried George, scribbling furiously in his exercise book. "Didn't you bellow some smoke and sparks in his face?"

"I couldn't manage a puff or a spark," admitted Sniffy, shamefaced. "All that came out was a huge sneeze, my cold having turned into 'flu. The force of the sneeze blew St. George from his horse. He was carried away on his shield to recover in the nearest castle. The people hated me for humiliating their hero. And so I decided to run away, and here I am."

"That's another lie the history books tell us," said George angrily. "St George didn't kill you at all. He was in bed in a castle with a bad cold. By the way, Sniffy, I've pinched another bed-sheet from mum's linen-cupboard. Here, have a really good blow."

While Sniffy was honking into the sheet, George was having a good think. Then his idea came.

"I think we can cure your cold, Sniffy," he

said, slowly. "Then when you are fully recovered you can go back to your past and become the dangerous dragon you always wanted to be. They won't giggle and sneer when you start breathing red-hot flames at your old enemies. Are you magic enough to go back to your youth? Or have the continual colds sapped every magic spell you ever possessed?"

"I could still travel back through time a little way," said Sniffy. "But not that far if I developed 'flu on the way. Then I'd end up in limbo with a bad chest, too ill to care about going forwards or backwards through the years."

"So, your future or past is all down to my cure," said George. "In the meantime, what you need is somewhere safe to live, plus central heating. Tell me, is your magic still strong enough to turn you into something else?"

"I could probably turn myself into something small," snuffled Sniffy. "Nothing larger than a mouse, I'm afraid."

"Which is perfect for my plan," said George, excitedly. "Now listen carefully and don't ask questions. I want you to breathe some damp puffs of breath in my face. Go on, we're friends after all."

Puzzled, Sniffy obeyed, coughing from the effort.

"Now," said George, wiping his watering eyes. "I want you to curl out of sight in the bushes until I return in the morning. And while I'm away, if you ever hear any more clanking of armour it'll be our next-door neighbour mending his car. Have you got that?"

"Yes," said Sniffy mystified. "When you come back will you bring me another bed-sheet, only this one is soaked already . . ."

But his small friend was already racing home and was way out of earshot . . .

The next morning George sat sniffling and snuffling over his cornflakes.

"You've got a cold, my lad," said his worried mother, feeling his brow. "No school for you today. It's straight to bed while I call the doctor."

"Can I just nip out and get my pet mouse, mum?" begged George. "Only he's got a bad cold too. He can stay in my bedroom until we both get better. We'll be company for each other."

"What pet mouse?" frowned his mother. "Since when have you had a pet mouse?"

"Since our budgie died," George lied. "His cage was rusting away in dad's greenhouse. So I thought I'd buy a biology mouse from school who was in need of a home. I'm sure you saw him once. I'm sure you said he was very nice."

"Did I?" said his mother, astonished. "Well, if I did I did. Very well, go and get this mouse of yours, and wrap up warm."

But George was already tugging on his anorak and scarf and woolly hat and racing down the garden path to snatch the old budgie cage from the greenhouse, quickly vanishing into the woods. There in total secrecy a small bit of magic took place. The boy gasped as Sniffy suddenly clenched his claws and sqeezed his eyes tight shut. Immediately the huge dragon began to dwindle in size. All at once he was a perfectly shaped scientific white mouse, but a mouse with a very bad squeaky cold. Pushing the transformed Sniffy into the cage the boy raced for home . . .

"Well, young man," said the cheerful doctor, tapping George's chest. "It's a few days bed-rest for you."

"I've turned up the central heating, doctor," said George's mother. "And he's got a lot of fresh fruit."

"And who is this?" said the nice doctor, peering through the bars of the cage that stood on the bedside table. "He's a funny kind of budgie."

"He isn't a budgie he's a mouse," said George quickly. "He certainly isn't a dragon. He's just my friend Sniffy who appears to look like something else, sometimes."

"Well," said the doctor, his eyes twinkling. "Budgie or mouse or even a fierce dragon, your friend has a terrible cold judging by his wheezing and runny nose. I think we'd better treat you both."

"Medicine for Sniffy as well?" said George, delighted. "He'll be ever so grateful Doctor."

"Well, even dragons who aren't budgies and look like mice need to come in from the cold when their chests are bad," smiled the Doctor. He scribbled on his note-pad and handed the prescription to George's mother. "Just keep George and his dragon nice and warm. Rub their chests with this special dragon ointment, it will help clear their lungs. Oh, and plenty of fruit and a dose of Lemsip every night. The ointment might sting a bit, I'm afraid."

"We don't mind doctor," said George,

happily. "I'll rub it on both our chests if it will make us well."

"You know Sniffy does look a bit like a tiny dragon in the right light," said the doctor, his eyes twinkling again. "What if St George climbs in through your bedroom window to slay this dragon-mouse of yours?"

Sniffy in the budgie cage began to gulp and wheeze, his tiny eyes wide with fear.

"No, doctor," said George, shaking his head. "St George only lives in history books these days. The rattle of the dustbin lids don't frighten Sniffy any more. Anyway, I'll always be here to protect him from danger."

"You're a bit of a St George yourself, young man," smiled the doctor. "If I were a dragon I'd feel very safe with you, but I must go . . . more calls you know. I'll pop round in a few days to see how my patients are progressing. Goodbye, George, goodbye to the mouse who could be something else."

"Thank you, doctor," said George's mother as she saw him out. "And don't mind George and all his silly talk. He makes up the strangest stories."

"So did I when I was his age," said the

doctor with, a far-away look in his eyes. "But sadly *my* dreams about dragons never came true."

But George's dreams had come true. Now his concern was to get his friend better and to copy into his exercise book as many dragon stories as Sniffy could remember before they both returned to full fitness. There was plenty of time, days of it. Every night when the house was quiet George would rub their chests and dole out two equal doses of Lemsip which had a wonderful effect on their colds. No runny noses, no watering eyes, it acted like magic.

Then Sniffy would scurry from the budgie cage and become again a huge blue dragon with orange spots. He would curl his lithe body all round the room and over the furniture as he breathed out a few sparks and began to recount the many dragon stories he had learned down the years.

Every night he told George a new story, telling them slowly so that George could scribble them down in his book.

"I'm going to be a writer when I grow up, you see," said George. "And my first book is going to be about dragons. So please don't tell any lies, not even white ones, Sniffy."

But Sniffy would never lie to his small St George, for he loved him too much. And as they talked and scribbled and basked in the warmth of the central heating in their sickroom, outside the wind howled and the rain torrented down and as the lightning flashed one could almost see the ghost of a vanished St George, galloping through the eerie woods as if in search of an enemy . . . an enemy who had long since come in from the cold . . .

And so the stories began. The boy and the dragon glorying in their private closeness, bonded by sneezes and common nose-running, as the wealth of stories unfolded.

# The
# DRAGON
## Brothers

One stormy night in the Magic Forest two dragons found a baby under a bush. He was wrapped in a cloak and crying bitterly. Beside him lay a lady, her face white in death.

"The unknown lady is at peace," said the first dragon, pity showing in his yellow eyes. "But the child still clings to life. Let us take him home and raise him as our own."

"I agree," said his wife, breathing warm air

over their find. "If we can raise one son to become big and strong we can surely raise two. Handle the child gently for he's already precious to me."

Then with a gentle nose she scraped out a grave and buried the poor lady under the bush where she had died. And the storm dashed blue rose petals from the bush onto the mound of earth as if to mourn her.

Back home in the cave the baby was stripped of his sopping cloak and fed a rich broth of mushrooms and milk and healing herbs. Then he was tucked into the nest to share the warmth of his new brother. He fell quickly to sleep, lulled by a dragon lullaby that grieved for all sons who had died because dragons and humans could not live together in peace.

The flickering light from the ever-burning fire lit up the cave. The walls were hung with gold and jewels and the booty of battles hoarded down the centuries, for dragons prized such things. The fire also illuminated the finger-ring strung around the baby's neck on a twist of twine, it's blue-rose emblem stirring great troubles in the hearts of dragons. For it was the ring of a prince, of a dragon-slayer. But because

they loved their new son completely the dragons stifled their fears, refusing to see future danger in the face of an innocently sleeping child.

The dragon brothers grew big and strong. Many happy days they spent playing together in the sunny glades of the Magic Forest. Small animals and birds would flee in alarm when the brothers staged their mock duels.

"Beware my glittering sword lest it should pierce your heart, wicked dragon," the boy would cry, brandishing a blackthorn stick.

"Beware that I might burn you to a crisp with my fiery breath, puny human," his brother would roar, advancing in all his hugeness.

When dusk fell over the Magic Forest the tired but happy brothers would go home to the cave for their favourite meal of mushrooms and milk and healing herbs, for they were ever children at heart. And the twitching seasons brought new years to pass . . .

One stormy night in the Magic Forest when the dragon family were warm and dry in their cave, the parents called their sons before the ever-burning fire. Their anguish was plain in the flickering light as they spoke to their now grown sons.

"It is time," wept the wife to her dragon son. "Gaze into the flames and read your destiny. Alas, that it is yours alone, for your father and I would bitterly share it."

The puzzled young dragon stared into the glowing embers to read the pictures flickering there. And his mind was filled with a terrible truth. Without a word to parent or brother, he shambled out into the storm raging throughout the Magic Forest. He did not look back.

"Equally loved son," said the father dragon, turning to the bewildered dragon-boy. "Gaze also into the fire to see your destiny. And when you turn to go away, never turn your heart on us, your loving parents."

The boy, now a sturdy youth, stared into the flames as bidden. And he saw everything there. The wicked King, his mother, her flight with him from the castle to the Magic Forest. And the anger rose inside him.

"Take these as your birthright," said his father, his yellow eyes filling with tears.

Reaching, from the glittering wall he took a bright, sharp sword and buckled it about the waist of his son. Reaching again he took down the cloak they had found their baby in. As the folds fell clear from the boy's shoulders, plain to see was the blue-rose emblem adorning it. Green claws squeezing his hands, his weeping mother slipped the blue-rose ring on his finger. Now the task was quite complete . . . the dragon parents had no longer . . . sons.

"Never look back," they pleaded as their second child strode out into the storm-lashed, lightning-flashed dawn in the Magic Forest. In the wild weather the dragon-boy knelt at the grave of his mother beneath the blue-rose bush. Then rising, vengeance on his lips, he strode out of the forest until he could lift his eyes to see the castle on the hill. The Blue-Rose Castle of his father and fathers.

Up the hill he marched, his bright sword drawn to slash back what was rightfully his. But his brave heart sank when he saw the enemy that barred his way. It was his dragon-brother, acting out his own destiny with an equally heavy heart. Brother gazed at beloved brother. Could either slay the other? Could the babe who shared the warmth, and mushrooms and milk and the healing herbs that had made him big and strong, kill the one with the yellow eyes, the soul he loved best of all in the world?

"I command you, dragon, kill the usurper with your fiery breath," cried the wicked, cowering King. "As my slave and keeper of my gate I order you to send this impudent prince to Heaven, or Hell."

But the brothers had had their fill of destiny. They had gazed into the flames of the everburning fire and had been saddened to view. Joining as close as they once did in their nest they turned as one, striking down the wicked

King and his craven minions. Then, together as
brothers, they entered their kingdom to the loud
'hurrahs' of the now happy people. The Prince
of the Blue-Rose was home, Glory be . . .

"And thus time turns," sighed the dragon
parents in the cave in the Magic Forest. In the
ever-burning fire they looked at pictures, and
sighed again, but with relief . . . "let it always be,
let life always even the rights and the wrongs,
and God bless our dragon sons . ."

And the storm abated in the Magic Forest,
and the blue-rose bush grew strong to shed more
petals on the grave of a lady who had not, had
never died in vain.

# THE NUISANCE
## UNDER THE BRIDGE

∽

Josh and Matilda and Ruffles their pet pig set off for the forest across the river. They were half-way over the wobbly bridge that spanned the waters when a cheery voice caused them to stop.

"Good morning, dearies," said the dragon, poking his green-spotted head from under the bridge, his grin a yard wide. "And where are we off to this beautiful autumn morning?"

For a while the brother and sister were

speechless with astonishment. Ruffles managed a nervous grunt. Matilda finally recovered her speech. She decided that politeness was the best way to cope with nosy dragons.

"As a matter of fact we're going to the forest," she said. "I'm going to gather a basket of blackberries for my mother to make into a pie."

"And you, little man?" the dragon smirked at Josh

"If it's any of your business I'm going to chop wood for my mother's fire," snapped the boy.

"And you, pretty plump one?" smiled the dragon, eyeing Ruffles. "What is your errand this trotter-kicking morning?"

Ruffles uttered another nervous grunt that ended in a squeal as he tugged on his lead to go home.

"Ruffles is going to root for truffles," said Matilda, annoyed. "And now if you don't mind you are holding up our expedition with your chit-chat. Good morning to you . . ." and she ushered her angry brother and the terrified Ruffles across the creaking planks to the firmness of the forest shore.

"I adore blackberries and truffles," yelled the

gleeful dragon after them. "I'm licking my lips already. I'll see you when you get back."

"The impudence," murmured Matilda as they entered the forest. "Dragons lurking under bridges, indeed. And prying into other people's business too." But she soon forgot her anger as the green forest lifted her heart.

In the meantime the nuisance dragon had slid back under the bridge to tickle and tease the local trout.

Being so busy Matilda, Josh and Ruffles had almost forgotten the unpleasant meeting with the dragon on the bridge. The plentiful autumn meant that Matilda could fill her basket with juicy blackberries in no time at all. Ruffles was just as lucky with truffles. Matilda was soon snatching them from his mouth faster than he could gobble them down. The little pannier on his back was filled by the time Josh came out of the deep forest with a load of oak logs on his back. After working so hard they enjoyed a lunch of bread and cheese on a grassy picnic spot. Then it was time to make for home. They travelled fast for the children were anxious to see the delight on their mother's face when she saw the bounty they had collected. Ruffles kept up easily with them. His snout was drooling at the thought of the extra bowl of swill he would earn as a reward for not scoffing down every truffle he had grubbed up. As they neared the bridge the children burst into a favourite ballad:

"Hey nonny nay
There's a mouse in the hay,
But it stays in bed on Sunday . . ."

Even Ruffles grunted along for little pink pigs are partial to ballads. All in all a happier homeward bound threesome would be hard to find in the whole of Merrie England.

They arrived back at the bridge in late afternoon. Crossing the rickety planks was quite a task because of the heavy loads they carried. Half-way across their hearts lifted to see the smoke drifting from the chimney of their cottage. Then they were stopped in their tracks. It was the grinning nuisance dragon again.

This time he was sporting bright blue spots as he reared up from beneath the bridge. Attractive he might be, but his attitude was as nasty as ever as he sneered at the halted trio.

"Home are the hunters, I see," he giggled.

His triangular eyes widened as he noted their piled-up loads. "My, we have had a good day. Any chance of a sample, a taste?"

"Certainly not," snapped Matilda. "Go and find your own dinner. We didn't gather this food for greedy, idle dragons to enjoy."

"Surely he can spare a truffle or two," said the dragon, grinning at trembling Ruffles.

"Don't you dare touch Ruffles' truffles," warned Josh. "Go away and plague someone else's bridge."

"And if I refuse?" enquired the nuisance, heaving his huge dragon-body onto the planks to bar their way home. "What if I stay here forever?"

"Then we'll stay here forever too," said Matilda, stubbornly. "We won't give in to a bully. You may be big but we'll fight our way past if we have to."

"Who needs to fight?" the dragon smiled. "You can earn your way across the bridge if you're talented enough."

"How?" asked Josh.

"By winning three challenges I intend to throw down," was the reply. "Win and you can cross the bridge, fail and I'll eat all those blackberries and truffles. That will upset your mother who is waiting with her pastry-crust to make you a wonderful blackberry pie. And," he added, "I'll use that little pink pig as a tooth-pick."

"You smirking blackmailer," cried Matilda. "If your own mother could hear you now she would be ashamed to have raised a wicked son."

As she said these words a change came over the sneering dragon. He seemed to shrink a little and his bright colours turned a dull grey. But only for a second or two. He was soon his grinning and colourful self again. Then to make his threat plain he reached out a claw and speared one blackberry and one truffle and popped them into his toothy mouth. Then he reached out and tweaked the tail of their little pink pet causing Ruffles to squeal in terror.

"Very well," said Josh. "We'll take up your challenge. What is the first one?"

"Tell me a joke that will make me laugh," said the dragon. "But it must be a joke to make my sides split with laughter. Laughter has always puzzled me, you see. I've only ever sneered. So make me rock with mirth."

Sitting on his oak logs Josh patted his sister to

sit beside him. With Ruffles cowering between them the boy launched into a very funny joke. At least his father had thought it funny when he had told it to the family after a night spent in the tavern with his friends.

"There were these two court jesters," Josh began. "One was coming up the hill and the other was going down the hill. Before they bumped into each other they stopped. The jester coming up the hill said, angrily, 'What are you doing wearing my hat?' and the jester going down the hill said, 'And why are you wearing mine?' They could have stood arguing for ages. But as they were both in a hurry to entertain their kings they simply swapped hats and went on their ways . . ."

Matilda pretended to rock with laughter. "It's the way Josh tells them," she giggled. But she was frightened inside.

"So where's the punch line?" snapped the dragon. "Why aren't I curled up in belly-rumbling laughter?"

"But don't you see?" asked Josh, desperately. "The jesters were wearing the exact same hats. There was no need to swap them at all."

"Well I'm not amused," said the dragon,

sourly. "And you won't be amused to find out that you've lost your first challenge."

"So what's the next one?" asked an anxious Matilda.

"Arm-wrestling," said the dragon, leering wickedly. "Who reckons they can beat me at arm-wrestling?"

"But that isn't fair," protested the girl. "The size of you and the size of us; we don't stand a chance."

"I shall only be using one claw," said the dragon, holding up his pointing one. "So, who is prepared to match their strength against mine?"

Josh restrained his sister as she made to jump up from the logs. He was proud of his muscles built up by lots of wood chopping. He squared up to the claw that the grinning dragon offered. Seizing it with his strong right arm the boy strained to force it onto the planks of the bridge. Puffing and panting he was unable to move it an inch. The dragon merely giggled. Then suddenly tiring of the game he wagged his powerful claw, sending Josh sprawling on his back. There was no pity in the dragpm as the red-faced and humiliated boy limped back to sit on the logs beside his angry sister.

"We haven't done very well, have we?" mocked their tormentor. "And now prepare for the final challenge. Win this one and I'll allow you to take home one third of the blackberries and truffles. The whole pile of logs you can keep with my blessing."

"Well, a third is better than nothing," said Matilda, her arm around her shamed and angry brother. Ruffles had buried his snout in his trotters in the hope it would make him invisible to the fearsome nuisance. He was hoping the last challenge wouldn't involve a small pink pig. Thankfully it didn't.

"Dance," said the dragon, abruptly. "I want to know why the world loves dancing so. Why it makes them smile in a happy way. I want to know why I remain so stiff and cold while the world dances. So, make me sway with enjoyment."

This third challenge was Matilda's own. She took it on with confidence. Standing, she began to twirl on her toes on the planks of the bridge, her arms waving gracefully, her hands tossing imaginary flowers to her imaginary audience. She ended her performance with a gracious smile and a low curtsy. To her dismay the dragon remained stiff and cold and unmoved. She returned to sit on the logs beside Josh and with their pig hugged close, three sunken hearts knowing that this dragon would show no mercy. There was nothing they could do as he plundered the bounty they had gathered from the forest.

"I've never lost a challenge yet," he giggled, his grasping claw reaching out to scoop every last truffle from Ruffles' pannier, another claw emptying Matilda's blackberry basket. With a greedy chew and a swallow their mother's cooking ingredients were gone. Then grinning widely he slid back beneath the bridge, only his sneering face remaining as he watched for their reaction.

"How the whole world must hate you," cried Matilda, mopping her tears with the hem of her smock. "What a waste of life to spend it persecuting children and little pink pigs. I only hope that God leans down from Heaven and wags a warning finger in your ugly face."

"And I hope a bolt of His lightning zooms down and strikes your fat nose," shouted Josh, enraged. "And Ruffles feels the same."

Ruffles might have done but he had other things on his mind. Seeing that the bridge was

clear he made a dash for home, his empty
pannier flapping on his back, his squeals renting
the air. The dragon leered and sneered as the
forlorn children followed their pet home, the
oak logs the sole treasure of that day.

"Everyone must have a scrap of decency and
kindness in them . . . somewhere," said a
bewildered Matilda.

"Not that dragon," said Josh, shaking his
head. "I don't know how he's slept with his guilt
for hundreds and hundreds of years. He must be
completely without a soul."

"Or his soul is ready to burst," finished
Matilda. "But come, we have a lot of explaining
to do . . ."

Josh and Matilda and their parents made the best of the meagre supper that night. The children had explained about the nuisance dragon under the bridge and the challenges they had lost. Their father said he wasn't surprised. He had often stumbled across dragons while coming home from the tavern at night, and they were all nuisances. It would have been nice to have a taste of truffle in the rabbit stew and have blackberry pie for afters, but being a close loving family they agreed that all in all the supper had been very nice, much to mother's pleasure and relief . . .

For seven days the children avoided the bridge. Most of the time they spent in improving their reading and writing. Ruffles approved of that. He passed this blissful time wallowing in mud, the memory of the terrible dragon fading from his mind with every satisfied grunt. Then on the eighth day Matilda and Josh decided that the bridge was a bridge and made for crossing. Why should they be afraid, they angrily agreed. Anyway the nuisance had probably left to make a pest of himself on someone else's bridge. So with fearful Ruffles in tow they went down to the river to watch and listen. Nothing stirred.

There were no loud water splashes that a huge swimming dragon would make. And the bridge was empty  and as rickety as an old bridge should be.

"I think he's gone," whispered Matilda.

"It seems like it," said hopeful Josh. "So, shall we?"

"Why not," said Matilda, calming Ruffles who now hated all bridges, empty or full. They tip-toed over the creaking planks. Even Ruffles, which is quite a feat for a little pink pig. There was no sight nor sound of anything save for the birds hopping and singing. The relieved trio reached the other side and set off for the forest to gather the bounty of that beautiful autumn day.

Matilda's basket was soon heaped high with delicious gooseberries. Then she attended to her little pink pig. She managed to snatch enough mushrooms from his chomping mouth to over-flow his pannier too. Then Josh came striding from the trees with a load of holly boughs on his back. Their mother loved the smell of blazing holly, and he was a thoughtful son. After a small picnic on a fallen tree, their pet scoffing most of it, they agreed it was time to go home. They travelled fast for they were impatient to see the joy on their mother's face when she saw their piled-up bounty. Ruffles kept pace easily with the children for he was anxious to cross the too-quiet bridge as soon as possible. As they neared the bridge Josh and Matilda began to sing another snatch of their favourite ballad:

> "Hey nonny no
> There's a hare in the snow,
> But he's only mad on Monday . . ."

Their step was carefree and confident as they began to cross the bridge. They were half-way over when their hearts sank. Rearing up from beneath came the loathsome face of the dragon, this time bright green and with an even wider sneer than before. The three stood still, waiting for his nastiness. It soon came.

"I was going to leave but decided not to," he giggled. "So, are you pleased to see me?"

"We certainly are not," chorused the disappointed and angry children. Ruffles sank onto the planks of the bridge and buried his snout in his trotters again. He *knew* this would happen.

"And what have we here?" said the nuisance, poking a claw into their baskets. His ugly face lit up. "Gooseberries and mushrooms. My favourites. May I have a small sample?"

"This time you will steal nothing from us," shouted Matilda. "Neither by trickery nor strength. We three are prepared to die rather than give in to you."

"Why die?" smiled the dragon. "You can easily cross the bridge and live to tell the tale."

"How?" said Josh.

"By telling me a story," was the reply. "But there is a condition. The story must be about dragons, and it must make me cry. I've never been able to cry and I'd like to know what it's like. Fail to make me cry and I'll eat everything you've got and chase it down with that little pink pig," and he tweaked Ruffles' ear to make the little pet squeal.

"Very well," said Josh quickly. "We'll take up your challenge. Just leave Ruffles alone."

"I'm waiting," said the dragon, curling comfortably on the planks of the bridge. "And the story must start with, 'Once upon a time . . .' otherwise it won't be a real story."

The children spoke urgently together. They

agreed that Josh's talents lay in chopping wood
and listening to stories, not telling them. So the
dragon's challenge fell on Matilda. The girl
already had a story forming in her mind.
Though a made-up one she believed it would
contain a lot of truth. It was plain their enemy
loved to bully and sneer. It was also clear he
hadn't a kind bone in his body. Which meant
friendship was completely unknown to him.
And the girl shrewdly reasoned that he was
deeply unhappy because of it. So, sitting on the
cut holly boughs beside Josh, Ruffles nestling
between them, she began a story that would
make the dragon cry:

"Once upon a time in a faraway land lived
two nice dragons. As hopeful parents they were
delighted when one sunny morning a small
dragonette was born to them. But as the
youngster grew up it was clear he would never be
as nice as his parents. As soon as he was strong
enough he began to bully and sneer at them. He
rejected the love they offered him, scorning their
attempts to guide him into nice ways. He liked
to spend his days lounging in the sun behaving as
nastily as possible to the dragons passing by. He
became so filled with hatred for everything that

he took to sneering at his own reflection in pools . . ."

As the girl paused in her story she noticed the dragon watching her closely through diamond-hard eyes. His toothy jaw was still quirked in a grin but his tail was giving the game away. It was restlessly thrashing, sending bits of rotting bridge tumbling into the river below. Matilda's words were hitting home. Now it was her turn to put pity aside as she continued . . .

"Then came the day when the young dragon left home to make his own way in the world. His nice parents shouted goodbye again and again but their callous son turned his face away and ignored them. He set off with a fierce ambition to make the lives of everyone else on earth as miserable as possible. In no time at all he was bullying and sneering his way around the planet leaving tears and heartbreak in his wake. Often on clear nights he would squat on mountain tops and curse the stars for shining down on a dragon who despised their romantic nonsense. And his anger at the world and himself remained diamond-bright as he lumbered to and fro, picking quarrels and making mischief wherever he could . . ."

Sprawled along the planks of the bridge the dragon giggled, though nervously. He now knew that Matilda had guessed the truth and was telling his own life story. He hated to hear it, but listened silently. His lashing tail continued to clip bits of wood from the bridge as she went on, not sparing one detail of his horrible life . . .

"But the wicked dragon could never find contentment, not even in sleep. While others slept through their troubles he stayed wide-awake, cursing their comfortable beds and plotting more vicious business for the coming day.

And so his bitter life went on unchanging for many hundreds of years. He was unconcerned that he was the most despised dragon on earth, for he hadn't a soul to examine. Then one day the news reached him that his parents had died. On his death-bed his kindly father sent a last message to his rampaging son: 'Please snap out of this tantrum, my child, and pull your socks up. You can be nice if you want to . . .' which sent the dragon in to a bout of rage such as the cowering world has never witnessed. It was his guilt coming out, of course. But how could a born-to-be-wicked dragon be nice and kind when he didn't know how to be? Unable to change, he blundered through his ruinous life, dashing the hopes and dreams of everyone who got in his way. But always at the back of his mind was the image of his kind parents wishing him goodbye as he stormed away, his cruel face turned scorning to reply . . .'

Matilda paused again to notice that the dragon was doing a Ruffles. His once brightly coloured head had turned grey again, and was buried in his clawed paws. But the girl wasn't finished:

"Then one day after a thousand years of wasted wandering the dragon chanced upon a rickety bridge. He decided to camp underneath and become a thorough nuisance to the children who needed to cross over, to gather food and fuel from the forest. And the lives of children and their pet pig were plagued by his bullying and sneering. Though they tried to be kind and polite, all they received was more bullying and sneering and ridiculous challenges. But the children and Ruffles still hoped in their hearts that the dragon would discover the gift of kindness that surely must lurk in a corner of his black soul, that his hard heart would melt a little, and that his eyes would weep tears through the planks of the bridge onto the fishes below. That is the end of the heart-rending dragon story."

At this point Matilda was weeping openly, her tears dripping into Ruffles pannier of mushrooms. Josh was glaring at the dragon's bowed head, itching to biff him one. Ruffles wasn't tearful at all. His trotters were stamping the planks as his tiny eyes searched for a sliver of light between the dragon and the handrail of the bridge. All he needed was a tight squeeze to make a dash for home. Then all at once there was all the room he needed. To the amazement of the children the dragon raised his head from his paws, his diamond-bright eyes glittering with tears. Without a word he shifted his bulk to allow free passage to the smoking chimney of home. Then he bowed his head again.

"Excuse me, dragon," said Matilda, nervously approaching and tugging one of his floppy grey ears. "Did my story really make you cry? So you do have a nugget of soft centre after all."

"How I wish I could be forgiven for all the wrongs I've done," wept the dragon, raising his greyed head. "Your story has made me see the

error of my ways and now I hate myself. Go
home and enjoy your family supper. When
you've gone I intend to end it all. I'm going to
hold my nose and roll into the river for the fishes
to feast on my remains. And with my dying
gurgle I will be thinking of you enjoying your
rabbit-stew with mushrooms, followed by gooseberry tart."

"Which is as close to our supper as you'll
ever get," snapped Josh. "We just want to see the
back of you and your bullying sneer. I only hope
Matilda doesn't go soft-hearted and make you
one of her worthy causes. Which she will,
knowing her."

"If only I'd learned to make friends," sobbed
the dragon. "I'd be the best friend in the world
if I knew how to do it. I'd be your best friend,
because the river is very deep and cold, and
death is so lonely all alone."

"I believe there's a spark of goodness in this
dragon," said Matilda, firmly. "I think that now
he's seen the error of his ways and wants to make
friends he's entitled to a fresh start. Even someone as wicked as he deserves a second chance at
life."

Ruffles wasn't interested in a second chance.

He had been waiting ages for his first one. Spying the clear run across the bridge he made a squealing dash for home, his bobbing pannier spilling precious mushrooms into the river below.

"How can you see goodness in this dragon, Matilda?" said Josh, outraged. "What kind of son would ignore his mother and father when they shouted and waved goodbye? Now he wants to be forgiven and make friends with us. I speak for Ruffles and myself when I say . . . never."

"Try to be kind, Josh" said Matilda, gently. "If the dragon is truly sorry and wants to make amends then we must help him."

"Oh yes, please," begged the dragon. "Help me if you can."

"Then you must start your new life tonight," said Matilda. "When it gets dark I want you to climb to the top of the highest hill you can find and shout your regrets to the stars. And perhaps your many victims and your parents who art in Heaven will hear and forgive you. In the meantime you must practice your smile for I notice your permanent sneer has made your mouth lopsided."

"I will," said the dragon, smiling sweetly. "And pardon me, Matilda, but isn't that basket rather heavy for you? Perhaps you would allow me to carry it across the bridge for you?"

"Why thank you," said Matilda, pleased. "But I can manage quite well."

"Then perhaps I can help young Josh with his logs," said the dragon, clambering to his huge, flat feet, his smile beautifully warm.

"I've always carried my own logs," said Josh rudely.

"Well, anything you need doing just tell me," smiled the dragon. "That's what close friends are for after all."

"You aren't our close friend yet," said Matilda, firmly. "It takes a long time for friend-ship to grow. But when you've proved yourself and have received forgiveness from the stars, then we'll grow a lot closer. We might even invite you to live under our bridge for the rest of your life, and perhaps even be invited for supper at our house."

"What an honour," gushed the dragon. "And will you please convey my kindest wishes to your parents and little pink Ruffles. Now I intend to lie here and think about all the wicked things I've done in my life. Goodbye for now my hopefully soon-to-be, first best friends," and he buried his face in his claws and began to sob tears of both gladness and grief.

As the children walked home across the bridge they felt a bit puzzled. Was it possible that after living such a wicked life the dragon could change so quickly?

"Into a fawning creep," said Josh, scornfully.

"It is rather a complete turn-around," admitted Matilda. "But perhaps dragons are like that. Horrible for hundreds of years then, in the blink of an eye, niceness and kindness itself."

"Niceness and kindness can also be a nuisance if it's overdone," said Josh wisely. "Perhaps dragons are born nuisances who throw their energies this way then that . . ."

But now they were hurrying along the winding path to their cottage, a lovely smell wafting out of the open door, for their mother always had something simmering in her black cauldron. Rabbit or poached venison hopefully. The good lady was thrilled with the gooseberries and the holly boughs and the few mushrooms she had rescued from Ruffles' pannier. That night the family enjoyed a lovely supper, the mushrooms adding a nice tangy taste to the venison stew. And the gooseberry tart simply melted in the mouth. Retiring to bed that night the family were just drifting off to sleep when a huge head crashed open their front door.

"I've been forgiven for all my sins," bellowed the dragon, excitedly, the din causing the family cat to claw yowling up the chimney. "The stars all winked in approval as I gazed up and prayed, and I swear I saw the dear faces of my parents smiling and nodding down in a loving way."

Matilda had jumped out of bed. She was angry. "And my parents are frowning and shaking their heads while they should be asleep. Couldn't this have waited 'till morning, dragon?"

"I just needed to tell a friend," said the excited dragon.

"But not in the middle of the night," said Matilda. "That's the way you lose your friends. I'm very pleased that you found peace under the stars, but folk do need to sleep, dragon. Go back under your bridge and get some sleep yourself. Then when you wake up you'll feel refreshed to start your new way of life. Good night, and I'll see you in the morning."

As she firmly closed the door and heard his heavy clawed feet lumbering away she worried as she climbed back into her bed.

Had she been too harsh on him, the dragon who wanted so much to be a friend? She fell into a troubled sleep . . .

The family woke to a morning of chaos. Unable to sleep because of his new-found happiness the dragon was re-ordering their lives as a mark of his kindness and love. Mother and father and Matilda and Josh, plus the cat still up the chimney, coughed and choked in the plaster and brick-dust that rained down the ceiling. Then a large portion of roof caved in. Through it appeared the happy face of the now purple dragon to wish them good morning.

"I noticed you had a few loose tiles on your roof," he shouted down. "So I'm doing a few repairs. I won't have rain dripping down the necks of my friends for the sake of a few tiles. Oh, and I've bought a few logs for the fire."

The family stumbled outside. Their tiny small-holding now looked like a timber yard. Piles of oak trunks and holly boughs lay dumped on mother's prized herb garden. But there was much worse to come. Clumsily scrambling down from the ruined roof the dragon made a triumphant announcement.

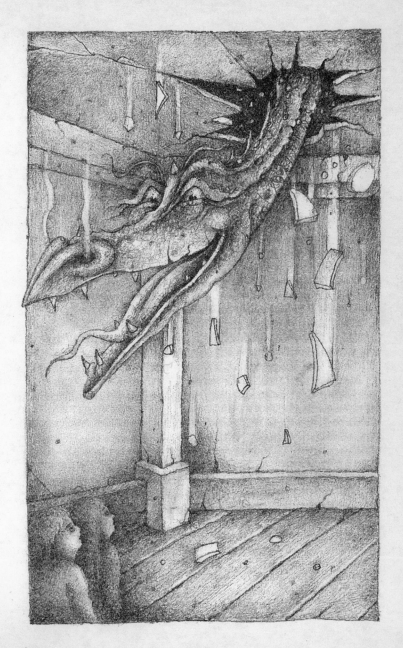

"Tonight I'm preparing supper," he said, his bright eyes dancing with delight. "We new friends are going to enjoy a feast indeed. The recipe is already slowly cooking in the barn. And for a special change it isn't chicken or rabbit or venison . . ."

He didn't need to say any more. With fear in their hearts Matilda and family raced to the barn. There they saw poor Ruffles lashed to a spit and squealing his little heart out as he revolved over a slow-burning fire. Matilda turned to the dragon to scream in anger as Josh rushed to free their singed pet from the trusses.

Then the girl saw . . . that the dragon was sneering again, his diamond eyes sharp with hatred.

"Do you really think you could have changed me?" he spat. "Do you really think I'd go into the high hills unless to hurl insults at the lying stars? Don't you see that my only love is hate?"

"And our offer of friendship meant nothing?" wept Matilda. "And yours neither?"

"Oh, it did for a while," said the dragon leering. "It offered me the chance to make your lives a complete misery, while pretending I had love in my heart."

"And you've succeeded in your wicked plan," said a miserable Matilda. "And me and my family and poor singed Ruffles will hate you for the rest of our lives. Each time we see your face on our bridge we will curse you."

"I'm afraid that pleasure will be denied you," sneered the dragon. "I think I've ruined the lives of your family about all I can. It's a new bridge for me, to make more mischief for new innocents. So, goodbye. Pity about the supper we never shared. Ruffles would have looked mouth-watering dished up in a rich gravy sauce, and with an apple in his mouth . . ."

And watched by the shocked parents and the angry children and their poor little whimpering pig, he vanished before their eyes, in fire and smoke, with a wide, echoing giggle.

"We have just watched the departure of the wickedest soul on earth," said Matilda.

"Perhaps the actual Devil in disguise," whispered mother.

"From evil to goodness, then back to evil," said Josh awed. "That takes a lot of nerve."

"He did say goodbye to a mother and father," said Matilda. "Our own."

"But he was sneering when he was saying it,"

said Josh. "So, goodbye to bad rubbish, I say. In fact that dragon was more nuisance being good. Just look what he's done to our roof."

"Which I'll have to mend," said father sadly.

"In the meantime there's food to prepare," said mother. "I've still got some rich stock for my cauldron. Would you children happen to be going across the bridge to the forest? The chest-nuts should be falling off the trees, and the damsons are ripe. And take Ruffles along. The walk will do his nerves good . . ."

And so the children set off for the bridge over the river for the forest. The outward journey was thankfully uneventful. But who could tell what lurked under any bridge? There would surely be more than one wicked dragon lurking about the world. The world was probably full of them.

Matilda and Josh and Ruffles sincerely prayed not. With fingers crossed they set foot on the bridge, every creak of its rotting planks causing them, especially Ruffles, to jump.

# THE
# DRAGON'S
### EGG

The three children were cycling through the old quarry when Bob's front wheel went wonky, plunging him down a steep slope. Jane and Harry peered over the edge praying he was only injured and not dead. To their relief Bobs' voice sounded up, not distressed but excited.

"You'll never guess what I've found," he shouted. "Tie your scarves together and pull me up. Have I got something to show you!"

Jane and Harry quickly lowered down their makeshift rope. Hauling it up they were not surprised to see Bob's bike tied to the end, it being his pride and joy. Next time, Bob came clambering over the edge covered in mud but with a wide grin on his face. Strangely he seemed to have grown a large stomach between falling down and coming back up. His tee-shirt bulged in the most peculiar way.

"So where's this great find then?" said Harry.

"Show us then," said Jane. "I hope it's more interesting than the broken ankle you could have had."

"How about this?" said Bob, triumphantly producing an oval-shaped object from under his tee-shirt.

"It's just an old rugger ball," said Harry, disappointed.

"A silly old rugger ball caked with clay," said Jane, disgusted. "It's probably been mouldering amongst those rocks for ages until you fell down and disturbed it."

"It could be the first rugger ball ever invented," said Harry. "You can always get a couple of quid for historic things in a car-boot sale."

"You haven't a clue what I'm holding, have you?" said Bob looking superior. "You may not know, but I subscribe to a monthly magazine called *The Dragons Are Amongst Us*, written by Professor Wildhair of Atlanta in America. While you were reading *Budgie the Helicopter*, I was seriously studying. Which is why I know exactly what this object is."

"It could be a dragon's Adam's-apple," smiled Jane. "The one an ancient dragon used to gulp with."

"Or a dragon's rugger ball," smirked Harry. "The game is as old as the world, they say."

"Scoff away," said Bob. "But in fact, what I'm holding in my hands is a genuine dragon's egg. Inside this lump of clay is a dragon who never hatched. Professor Wildhair of Atlanta, Georgia, America, says that millions of dragons never hatched from their eggs because they were eaten or squashed, or buried in cold swamps. He said if you find one you can always tell it's the genuine article by it's colour and markings. He said a dragon's egg is always blue and covered in bright silver stars."

Jane was scratching at the hardened clay. She looked surprised.

"Professor Wildhair could be right," she said. "There's blue underneath and a silver star is appearing."

"Maybe," shrugged Harry. "But why didn't the dragon hatch out?"

The professor said that dragons' eggs need lots of steamy heat to incubate," said Bob. "Obviously this egg has been lying dormant in cold rocks and swamp for thousands of years. It never had the chance to hatch."

"Plenty of steamy heat, eh," said Jane. "Well that's no problem. We can pop the egg in my dad's greenhouse behind his tomatoes. He'll never see it. He has to check the growth of his tomatoes by feel because the steam mists up his glasses, so the egg would be perfectly safe."

"That's solved then," said Bob, pleased. "Let's get the egg properly cleaned up and wrap it in Harry's tee-shirt away from prying eyes. Then we will seize our chance to sneak it into the greenhouse."

"Why my tee-shirt?" Harry protested.

"Because I found the egg, Jane provided the greenhouse, while you've done absolutely nothing," explained Bob. "This is a three-way project so if anything goes wrong we all share the blame. We'll also share the fame, if it comes," he added.

It was agreed. Minutes later they were pedalling for Jane's dad's greenhouse. Sneaking inside they tucked away the dragon's egg in the steamiest corner. Then after a clever disguise job with the tomato leaves they went their separate ways, home for Sunday tea.

They met after school for the next two weeks to inspect the dragon's egg. Though it was warm and nicely bathed in steam it remained the same. It was frustrating to watch the tomatoes growing plump and red while their dragon's egg showed not one sign of life. Then came another Sunday.

"I still say it's just a lump of coloured rock," said Harry, wiping the sweat from his brow. "So much for Professor Wildhair. If I were you Bob, I'd cancel that magazine and demand my money back."

"I can't," said Bob. "Professor Wildhair sends a personal letter to every member stating that he can not supply refunds. That's because every cent we send goes straight into The Dragon Academy he's building."

"Into his big posh house with the swimming

pool, you mean," said Harry, scornfully. "You've been had, Bob."

"Be quiet a bit," hissed the girl. She was munching a Mars bar and gazing intently at the egg. "I'm sure it's lighting up inside. And I'm sure there's something moving."

The boys stared. She was right. The egg had become transparent and there was something newt-like clawing at the wall of the shell. But it was the eyes of the tiny creature they could see through the shell that shocked the children most. They were blood-red and staring fixedly at Jane.

"I don't think I like this," she shivered. "What have we done . . . ?"

Suddenly the egg split into two even halves and out sprang a small dragon. It had to be a dragon. It had an overlarge head and flaring nostrils and a zig-zag crest running from the top of its head to the tip of its tail. Its colour was amazing. Rainbow stripes adorned its body making it look like an expensive bulls-eye sweet from Harrods. Its red eyes never left Jane as it suddenly darted forward. The girl screamed as the remains of her Mars bar were snatched from her hand. Just as swiftly the dragon vanished behind the greenhouse pipes.

For a few seconds the sound of scoffing could be heard. Then the dragon re-appeared, looking twice as big and licking his toothy chops. This time its restless eyes focused on the bag of crisps Harry had bought along for a snack. Quick as a blink it flashed and dashed out a clawed paw. One gulp and the crisps were gone, packet, and all.

Then the eyes turned on Bob. But the boy who had found the dragon's egg had already thrown his cheeseburger into the dragon's mouth and was haring from the greenhouse, Harry and Jane close on his heels.

Pausing for breath at the garden gate they looked back.

"It isn't possible," gasped Jane, staring.

"Is it my eyes?" said Harry in disbelief. "Though it should be impossible."

It might have been the sunlight shimmering on the steamy glass of the greenhouse and distorting the image inside. Yet it seemed that the once tiny dragon now filled the inside with its swelling bulk. Suddenly there came an ear-splitting sound of breaking glass and the children were racing in panic down the lane. They headed for the refuge of the giant elderberry bush in

Harry's garden that served as a den and a place to think.

"We could be dreaming," whispered Bob, "Professor Wildhair said that people dream about dragons all the time."

"So where's my Mars bar?" said Jane.

"And my crisps," said Harry. "The hard truth is there's an expanding dragon on the loose in our village, and it's all the fault of Bob and Professor Wildhair. In my opinion the professor should be jailed in Atlanta Prison for bringing mayhem to quiet English villages, and Bob with him." He glared angrily at his friend.

"My dad will go spare when he sees his greenhouse smashed to smithereens," wept Jane. "Why did you do it Bob?"

"Do what?" said Bob, indignantly. "I didn't smash it. I only saw with my own eyes what you saw with yours. Anyway, who volunteered the greenhouse, and who delivered the egg there under his tee-shirt?"

"Alright," said Harry wearily. "We're all to blame. So what do we do?"

"We've got no choice." said Jane. "We've got to face the music. We've got to go back to my house and see what's happened."

Back at Jane's house her dad was ranting and raving amidst the ruins of his beloved greenhouse. The children looked shocked and said sympathetic things. But all the time their eyes were darting. They were relieved to note no sign of the dragon or his shattered egg.

"A strange thing happened to me an hour ago," said Jane's mum bewildered. "I made a pink strawberry blancmange for Sunday tea. I put it by the open window to cool and the minute my back was turned it was gone. All that was left was the plate with a large chunk bitten out. It was definitely bitten, for the teeth-marks are here to see. Look."

"Have you three been up to something?" asked Jane's dad looking keenly at the children. "I've 'phoned the village policeman and he's coming round to investigate. I hope you aren't involved in this vandalism in any way."

"We're studying for exams, dad," Jane protested. "We haven't got time to be vandals. We're as sad about the greenhouse and mum's blancmange as you are."

"A freak hurricane could have smashed the greenhouse," suggested Harry. "They have freak hurricanes in the South Seas every day."

"Or," said Bob, "you could have a rival tomato-grower in the village who's jealous of all the cups in your trophy case."

"Maybe," said Jane's dad, not convinced. "We'll wait and let the police sort it out."

"And I did so want you to enjoy my strawberry blancmange," said sad, Jane's mum.

"And we so wanted to taste it," said the three.

"Oh well," said Bob. "School in the morning. Better be going."

"Me too," said Harry. "Monday morning exams and all that."

The boys slunk away, their fingers crossed. Perhaps the rampaging dragon had moved on to create havoc elsewhere. Judging by its speed and its sweet tooth it could easily have dashed across the channel to Belgium where they made the best chocolates in the world. But the main thing was that the dragon had gone, so where was the evidence against them?

"Traitors," hissed Jane after the disappearing boys. But she also felt let off the hook. With the dragon gone, even if the police took finger prints they could never connect her to this particular crime.

Monday, exam Monday. Everyone hated ordinary Mondays.

The questions were hard and the answers were even harder, and worry occupied the minds of most children that testing morning. There was no spare bit of brain to think about anything else. Bob, Harry and Jane had almost forgotten the dragon affair of the previous day. Like everyone else they were clicking their biros and gazing at the ceiling in search of inspiration. It was a tremendous relief when the bell rang for lunch break.

Lined up with their trays the children gazed hungrily at the hot-plate choices spread before them. There were trays of succulent brown sausages, vats of bubbling baked beans and heaps of crispy golden chips. Here they were all brilliant at maths. With a glance they could calculate the exact number of chips on a neighbour's plate which lead to some squabbling. Meanwhile the ladies behind the hot-plates fumed and threatened to crack their cheekier kids over the head with their ladles. There was always a fast sliding past the cabbage and carrots and sprouts to the pudding counter. Like art critics the children admired the colour and design of apple crumble, raspberry tart and bread-and-butter pudding. This was indeed the happiest time of the school day. It was about to become a time the children would never forget. The line had barely shuffled to the sausages when the wall of the canteen caved in amidst a thunder of tumbling bricks and falling masonry . . .

For a moment the bulls-eye striped dragon stood wreathed in a cloud of dust, its red eyes roaming. It soon spied what it sought. With a delighted bellow it lumbered to the counter, its huge paw sweeping the children aside like chaff. While the terrified ladies buried their faces in their aprons the dragon began to strip the hot-plates bare of sausages to raspberry tart, leaving only the cabbage and the carrots and the brussels-sprouts. Stuffing everything into its huge mouth, it upended the orange-juice urn and gurgled it dry. Then with a mighty burp it vanished as fast as it arrived.

There was a stunned silence in the wrecked canteen. Then tears began to flow as covered in dust and sprayed chip-fat the children and the ladies began to comfort one another.

"The dragon was a mile high, honest," wept the small girl to the village policeman who arrived in his car with Snuffer his sniffer dog. "And it was striped like a bulls-eye with nasty red eyes, and ate all the chips."

Consulting his notebook the policeman immediately linked the canteen outrage to the destruction of Jane's dad's greenhouse. Two strange events in one day surely had to be more than a coincidence. Ambitious to be posted from the village to Scotland Yard he ordered the suspect three into the Head's study where he had set up his crime-room. With Snuffer guarding the door, the frightened three were soon confessing . . .

"So you found the dragon's egg in the old quarry," nodded the policeman. "And you smuggled it into Jane's dad's greenhouse to hatch. And when it did hatch and ran amok you pretended to know nothing about it. Is that your story?"

"It's all the fault of Bob's dragon magazines," wept Jane. "Professor Wildhair keeps sending them every month."

"Professor Wildhair who lives in a big house in Atlanta, Georgia," agreed Harry. "With a deep blue pool to swim in."

"No, I'm to blame," said Bob, ashamed. "I

was the one who persuaded Harry and Jane to help hatch the egg. Professor Wildhair only explained how to do it."

"Professor Wildhair of Atlanta, Georgia," scribbled the policeman in his notebook. "That will be America, of course. And is the dragon as tall as I've been told, like a mile high?"

"No," said Bob. "Nowhere near that."

"In the beginning it was about as big as a newt," explained Jane. "But after it scoffed my Mars bar and Harry's crisps it was twice as big. It seems to grow bigger with everything it eats."

The policeman closed his notebook and pointed his pencil at Bob. "Well, young man, we are going to send some urgent telegrams to your Professor Wildhair asking him what to do about a dragon running wild in the English countryside. As an expert he must know the answer."

"A better answer would be to call the SAS," said Harry. "They could float down on parachutes and throw a big net over the dragon. Then they could blow it away with their stun grenades!"

"This is a village problem," said the policeman, hastily. "We don't need outsiders to solve it. Me and Snuffer are well on top of the case.

We'll soon track down this dangerous dragon. It will soon find out there's no hiding place from Snuffer's nose."

"If I were a huge dragon I'd hide in the old disused railway tunnel," said Harry. "I think we should search there first."

"We'll need new batteries for our torches," said the excited Jane. "The old tunnel is very dark even in daylight."

"As your deputies, do we get to wear badges and carry truncheons?" Harry asked the policeman. "And do we get to hold Snuffer's lead?"

Snuffer gave a short angry bark.

"Snuffer only allows *me* to touch his lead," said the policeman firmly. "What I need from you are the two halves of the dragon's egg. Snuffer can't begin tracking without some clue to sniff at."

"That's easy," said Jane. "My mum found them in the ruins of the greenhouse. They were such a pretty blue she arranges flowers in them."

"Run home and bring them back for Snuffer to sniff," ordered the policeman. And to Harry he said, "You go with her. And be sure to pat Snuffer as you go through the door or he might arrest you as escaping criminals."

Jane and Harry paused to pat the police-dog as they raced from the crime-room. "Now my lad," said the policeman to Bob. "We are going to send a fax message to your Professor Wildhair. You will accompany me and Snuffer to the station. And don't get into the front seat of the car unless you want to be hurt. Snuffer sits there."

At the station the fax was swiftly composed and sent. It read:

## URGENT:

TO:      Professor Wildhair, *THE DRAGONS ARE AMONGST US* Magazine
Atlanta, Georgia
United States of America

*Dragon's egg found in England. Has hatched out as per your instructions. Dragon now fifteen feet tall and rampaging around village stealing sweets and puddings and chips. The dragon has red eyes and is striped like a bulls-eye sweet. Please send solution to this terrible problem before said village is utterly destroyed by this dragon you caused to hatch.*

SIGNED:      Snuffer of Scotland Yard

"That's a bit of a white lie, isn't it?" grinned Bob. "After all, Snuffer is only a village sniffer dog."

"More like a big lie," smiled the policeman. "But if any dog deserves to be a member of Scotland Yard, Snuffer does. And when he tracks down the dragon and brings it to justice, I'll be holding its lead in all the photographs. After all a skilled sniffer dog goes nowhere without its master."

Professor Wildhair's reply arrived that same day. His prompt fax was spurred by the world-wide fear of Scotland Yard. He said he was sending the solution to the dragon problem by special air-mail. He advised that the solution should be placed as near to the dragon's nose as possible. He also stressed that the two halves of the egg should be kept close by.

In the meantime, after a quick sniff at the egg-shell, Snuffer led the policeman and the children to the mouth of the old railway tunnel. Harry was right. Shining their torches into the gloom they couldn't mistake the huge bulk of the bulls-eye striped dragon, crouched on the rusty rails, its red eyes glowing like warning lanterns. Suddenly it began to roar, the blood-curdling sound echoing around the tunnel. Everyone fled, Snuffer leading the way with his tail between his legs, and howling. Back at the station Jane asked the policeman a question.

"Don't you think that you should call in the real Scotland Yard?"

"Or the SAS?" said a hopeful Harry.

"Certainly not!" snapped the policeman. "This is a village matter. Snuffer and I can handle it. Anyway, Professor Wildhair's solution will be arriving by air-mail in a couple of days . . ."

But a couple of days would be too late for some people.

In the village High Street stood a row of shops. One was called The Candy Shoppe and belonged to Mrs Timms who sold every kind of sweet in the world. She also sold every flavour of crisp, including roast-beef-and-honey flavoured. Next door was the greengrocer who sold carrots and sprouts and cabbages. Next door to him was the butchers. The butcher always wore a straw hat and grinned out of his window while sharpening his silver knife. Next door down was the Mr Lazio's ice-cream parlor and milk-shake bar. But it was the last shop in the row that was the

village's favourite. This was Georgio's Fish and
Chip Emporium. Here the children liked to
gather after school to gossip and pinch each
other's chips  before going home to hopefully,
more chips . . .

The raid was sudden and brutal. That
afternoon while people strolled in and out of the
shops excitedly discussing the latest dragon news,
into the High Street it lumbered. Cars were
tossed aside like Dinky toys as the dragon
advanced along the central white line of the road,
its roars causing fainting fits and frantic fright.
The terror of the railway tunnel had come
shopping . . .

Mrs Timms was the first to suffer. With a
swipe of a clawed paw it demolished her shop
front. Poking its head inside, its red eyes
surveyed what Mrs Timms had hoped to sell.
But the dragon wasn't buying. It began at the
chocolate counter. Everything from chocolate
buttons to ribboned boxes of chocolate truffles
were stuffed into its gaping mouth. Then it
turned to the jars of boiled sweets and toffees.
Gulping and swallowing down they went, jars
and all. The assorted crisps were still in cartons.
No problem. Into that gobbling mouth they

went, cardboard and all. Satisfied that Mrs Timms' shelves were stripped bare the dragon turned and shambled down the street to Mr Lazio's, ignoring the greengrocers and the butchers inbetween. There it began another ferocious binge. Down its greedy throat slid tubs of multi-flavoured ice-cream and packets of mixed-nut topping. Licking up the dregs from the floor, it turned and moved on down the street.

Having seen what was happening, Georgio dashed inside his fish-shop and bolted his door, desperately turning the sign to CLOSED. But the tempting smell of frying drifting from under the door made his siege futile. The dragon didn't even glance at the CLOSED sign as it smashed through the plate-glass window. Licking its lips it attacked the piles of freshly-fried golden chips and battered fish and the steaming cauldron of mushy peas. Tossing the lot down his throat, it topped up with a giant jar of pickled onions. Then plunging its huge nose into the pans of sizzling fat it slurped them dry. Turning about it left the fish-shop and waddled further down the street in the direction of the railway tunnel, poor Georgio shouting Greek curses at its bulls-eye striped back.

But suddenly a beautiful smell caused its nose to twitch and its paws to mark time. Its roving eyes focused on a tucked-away building at the end of the street. It was Mr Smith's Bread and Cakery Bakery that catered for people who hated sliced loaves. Crashing inside the dragon gorged down every stick of French bread and fancy pastry freshly-baked that day. Then tossing down a wedding and two birthday cakes it lumbered towards the railway tunnel to sleep off its heavy meal.

In the meantime the terrified villagers hurrying home began to phone the police-station to report that their fridges and deep-freezers had been ripped open and stripped of everything but frozen vegetables. They were so angry that Snuffer and the policeman feared they would never make it to Scotland Yard. In short their twosome team had fallen down on the job.

"And you promised me a nice bit of steak for my supper," said Bob's dad to Bob's mum, sighing. "I was looking forward to that after a hard day."

"Blame your son," said the lady, sharply. "If he'd left that dragon's egg well alone our village would be as normal as usual. Now all we've got is chaos."

"It's Professor Wildhairs fault," muttered Bob. "Because of him that dragon has eaten all our fish-fingers."

"Just be quiet and eat your boiled carrots," snapped his mum. "And think yourself lucky Scotland Yard hasn't been brought in, otherwise you'd be under close arrest."

For the next fourty-eight hours the phone in the police-station rang constantly. Every call was a complaint. The dragon was now ambushing food-delivery vans, and one tiny girl had even been mugged in her pram as she sucked on her milk-bottle. The dragon was now snatching milk from babies . . . and what was the policeman and his 'talented' Snuffer companion going to do about it?

"The solution to our dragon problem is on the way," he shouted desperately down the 'phone. "Just trust me and Snuffer."

But Snuffer had slunk into the station's prison cell where he refused to eat his bowl of Chum as he howled his hatred for the dragon who had ruined his Scotland Yard career.

Then like manna from Heaven Professor

Wildhair's solution arrived. It was in the shape of a cardboard box bound with sticky tape. Stripping away the wrapping the policeman drew out what looked like a large blue egg decorated with silver stars.

"That's just another dragon's egg," said Bob angrily. "What kind of solution is that? We've had enough trouble with the first dragon's egg we found."

"I was hoping Professor Wildhair would have posted a guided missile," said Harry disappointed. "Then we could have zapped out the dragon with fire-power."

"But it smells nice," said Jane, leaning to sniff. Then she grinned. "And it's even nicer to lick. I think I know what this solution is. It's a replica dragon's egg that changes colour when you lick it, and gets smaller and smaller until there's nothing left but the taste."

"Like a giant bulls-eye," said the bewildered policeman. "And what did the professor instruct us to do?"

"To place the solution as close to the dragon's nose as possible," read Bob aloud.

"And to keep the two halves of the original egg-shell close by," added Jane. "The professor says this is very important."

"So, let's do it," the policeman shrugged. "We've nothing to lose. Mine and Snuffer's careers are down the tube anyway."

Then came a howling from the prison cell as the four set off for the dragon's lair in the tunnel. Snuffer was afraid he was going to be retired from the police force because of cowardice. He was frantic to solve the case of the dragon and win a medal from the Queen. With a clever paw he unlocked the cell door and raced after them.

Clutching the giant blue sweet, Bob ventured into the gloomy railway tunnel. Close behind crept Jane and Harry, each hugging one half of egg-shell. Alongside them strode the policeman, his powerful torch lighting the way, his truncheon drawn.

They were joined by a panting Snuffer determined to be in on the arrest. On stealthy paws he crept along behind the party as they advanced into the unknown.

The dragon was sleeping off its latest huge meal, its head in its claws, its snores echoing around the dripping walls of the tunnel.

At a sign from the policeman Bob stole

forwards and placed the starry blue egg by the tip of the dragon's nose. Then he raced back to join the others. After a minute or two the dragon opened its eyes and stared at Professor Wildhair's solution. Cautiously it flicked out a long tongue and licked. Then it licked again. A look of bliss came over its ugly face. It was as if all the most delicious flavours in the world had come together in this wonderful confection. The dragon licked on, the giant sweet shrinking and changing colour through different shades of blue and ever-shifting stars before its wide red eyes.

But something else was happening . . .

"Look, the dragon is shrinking too," gasped Jane.

"And changing colour, just like the sweet," said Harry, awed.

It was true. As the sweet egg shrank, so did the dragon. It was as if each was devouring the other. A few more minutes passed, then . . .

"The dragon is almost  as small as when he hatched out from his egg," shouted Bob. "And the professor's solution is practically licked to nothing."

"Right, this is where I make my arrest," said the policeman, snatching the two halves of shell and marching down the tunnel.

The tiny dragon just managed to utter an angry squeak before it was clapped between the halves of its own shell. Handing it to the children to hold tightly he drove them all at breakneck speed back to the station. Once there the egg was sealed with superglue. Peering inside the starry blue egg the children felt quite sad to see the little dragon clawing at the inside in its desperation to get out. But wise to the wiles of dragons they all knew how easily a free one could destroy whole villages and force the population to survive on horrible turnip soup.

"Now," said the grim policeman. "I'm ordering your three to get on your bikes and bury that dragon's egg where you found it. And just in case you're tempted to disobey, I'm sending constable Snuffer along to make sure the law is carried out. In the meantime I've got an important report to write to my Chief Constable about a case brilliantly solved and closed."

Snuffer was full of his old zip as he escorted the three bikes back to the old quarry, treating the children like unruly sheep. Sitting on his haunches his keen eyes watched every move as Bob was lowered down the steep drop. Soon the dragon's egg was sealed back into the tomb in which it had been found and packed around with rocks and swampy clay, to stay locked away, hopefully for evermore. Or until some day in the future when other children fall down the steep drop and make the discovery all over again. With Snuffer bounding ahead the children rode back to the village, lost in thought, often sad. But they soon cheered up when they noted that the shops were having new dragon-proof windows fitted, and the delivery vans were busily unloading sweets and ice-cream and other essentials to re-stock the shops.

The three weren't surprised when the policeman and Snuffer were given medals and left the village to become Scotland Yard detectives. Though they were sad to see them go.

However, the new policeman seemed very nice. And his puppy dog was called Sniffler.

The dragon affair soon became a memory. A nightmare memory that woke people in the small hours of the morning. But only a memory, for the real thing was buried under mounds of rock and clay. The tiny dragon was safely imprisoned and hopefully would remain so for the rest of time. But the rest of time is a long while. And in the meantime the dragon crouched in its egg-shell in the darkness, waiting, always waiting . . . for freedom.

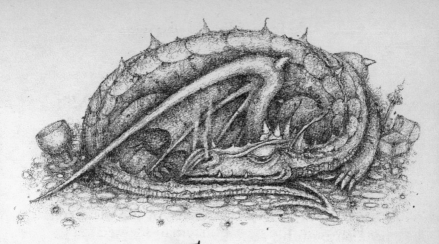

# ERIC
## AND THE
## DRAGON TWINS

E ric was droving his sheep up to higher
pasture when he came upon the entrance
to a cave. For a moment his eyes were
dazzled by the heap of gold and gems sparkling
in the sun. Curled on top of the hoard was an
orange dragon with smoking nostrils and a nasty
gleam in his eye.

"Good morning," said Eric, politely. "It's a
lovely day to be droving sheep. It's a lovely day
to be a rich dragon, no doubt."

"Don't smarm me with your lovely days," bellowed the dragon. "I know what you're after. Touch one golden piece and I'll make a bonfire of you. I need every speck of this treasure to bring me the luck I missed out on when I was small. And in case you haven't got the message, try a taste of this . . ."

Pursing his mouth the dragon aimed a stream of sparks at Eric's sheepskin breeches, scorching the wool clean off.

"I may be poor but I'm not a thief," said Eric, angrily. Patting at his hot ruined breeches, he said, "anyway, precious gold and jewels don't always bring luck. Looking and listening to you I sense a very unlucky dragon. Lonely too. I think you only bellowed at me because you wanted company. Am I right in guessing you haven't the luck of friends?"

The dragon bowed its orange head, his tears splashing on green emeralds and blood-red rubies.

"I thought so," said Eric, crooking a straying lamb. "I think it's time you pulled yourself together and made a go of life. I suggest you slither off that pile of treasure and go out and meet other dragons. There must be another dragon you'd like to meet with and talk to. If only to talk about the weather and price of gold. Then you'd have the warmth of a friend instead of the coldness of diamonds. What do you say, you miserable old bellower?"

The rich dragon burst into tears as he told his sad tale, his nose merely steaming now.

"I do have a twin brother who lives higher up the mountain," he mourned. "But on the day we were born he did a terrible thing. Because of that we haven't spoken for ten thousand years."

"Good heavens," said Eric, astonished. "He must have done a really terrible thing to part you for all that time. What did he do?"

"On the day that we were born our grandma gave us each a lucky coin," sobbed the dragon. "As we grew older I came to love and trust my brother totally. I thought he loved me too. Then one day he ran away with both coins and never came back."

"Why didn't you wake up and run after him?" said Eric, outraged.

"Because while I liked to sleep a lot he liked to practise his secret running," was the sad reply. "One morning when I woke he was long gone with the lucky coins. Since that day his treachery has nagged away inside my head. Why did he do it? I could never understand. He was my brother and my only friend, you see. That's why I bellow at nothing a lot. That's why I bellow at scruffy shepherd boys who climb into my mountains. Any company is better than none at all."

"I may be scruffy but I'm clean," snapped Eric. But his kind heart went out to the lonely dragon. Crooking close the lamb who loved to stray he thought a lot as shepherd boys do. Then the idea came. "We're going to solve your problem, orange dragon. We're going to find out exactly why your twin ran off with your luck as well as his own. Which means you must stir yourself. I want you to slide from that treasure and go up the mountain to thrash everything out with your twin. I realise that meeting after ten thousand years will be awkward, but this is no time for shyness. You must confront the hated brother who is eating away at your soul. Don't worry about your golden jewels, I'll look after them while you're away."

"I knew it," raged the dragon through more floods of tears. "Shepherd boys are as treacherous as twins. I know your plan. As soon as my back is turned you'll steal every last speck of the treasure I'm hoarding to bring me the luck I deserve."

"I won't warn you again," said Eric with dignity. "I may be a poor shepherd boy but I'm not a thief. One more remark like that and I'll leave you in the unlucky state I found you in."

"Anyway," said the dragon, huffily. "Why should I climb the mountain to see him? He's the thief who stole my lucky coin. If my twin wants my love back he must return the luck he stole from me and apologise on his bended knee."

"I never knew that orange dragons could be so stubborn," sighed Eric, uncrooking his mischievous lamb. "But very well, as I am determined to bring you twins back together I'm going to act as your go-between. Luckily for you I just happen to be going your brother's way."

And gently crooking his sheep together he began to drove them to higher, more succulent pasture.

"Remind my wicked twin that our grandma loved us equally," bellowed the dragon after him. "Remind him that she willed one coin to me. Force him to bring back my luck with his head bowed low."

Later, and higher in the mountains, Eric sat on a rock to munch his bread and cheese and think a lot as shepherd boys do. Suddenly the peace was shattered by a deafening bellow. Startled, Eric turned to notice the mouth of another cave. Squatting at the entrance was another orange dragon with smoking nostrils and a nasty glint in his eye. But this dragon was curled up on nothing more than bare earth and gravel. He was obviously very poor.

"Good morning," said Eric, crooking his wanderlust lamb. "It's a lovely day to be a poor shepherd boy in charge of healthy sheep. I expect it's a lovely day to be a healthy dragon, poor as you are. You and I should give thanks for what we've got, even though it's not a lot."

"Why should I offer thanks for nothing?" bellowed the dragon. And drawing in breath he whooshed a jet of flames at Eric, scorching the boy's sheepskin tunic almost from his back.

"That's what I get for being friendly," coughed Eric, angrily. "That's a new tunic you owe me, you bad-tempered old bellower."

"Buy you a new tunic?" said the poor dragon, bitterly. "Earth and gravel is all I own in the world. Your luck is out, little shepherd boy, for luck was never a friend of mine."

"If you'll stop being violent I could be a friend," said Eric, ever kind and willing to forgive. But as your new friend I must tell the truth. I've just been talking to your rich twin down the mountain and he reckons you're a dyed-in-the-wool villain. Yet in spite of his huge wealth he's just as lonely and unhappy as you. The only thing that keeps him going is the hope that one day he can wring your orange neck for running away with two helpings of luck while he was trustingly fast asleep. He's very angry that you never let on you were a champion sprinter."

"Didn't my twin say one nice thing about me?" whispered the poor dragon, his clawed paws wringing anxiously. "Didn't he say that blood was thicker than water, and that he still loved me in spite of my wickedness?"

"I'm afraid not," said Eric, shaking his singed head. "But there is one tiny gleam of hope for you. Your twin just might forgive you if you crawl into his presence on bended knee, blubbing you apologies."

"Creep and crawl, never," bellowed the poor dragon. "I know I did wrong all those thousands of years ago, but I've suffered too. For one tiny mistake my twin wants me to creep and crawl? Never."

"It was hardly a tiny mistake," said Eric, gently. "You did run away with his treasured coin. And I can see from your poverty that all your life those lucky coins have been turning up tails instead of heads. That's probably your grandma's curse."

"Oh, the bad luck I've suffered," wept the poor dragon, facing at last the terrible thing he had done. "But I was young and greedy, and had learned to run early. I ran away determined to be the richest and most important dragon in the world. But grandma's luck turned sour on me. For just look at me now, sitting on nothing while my twin sits on huge wealth."

"I am looking, poor dragon," said Eric, sadly. "It's a funny old world. You were born with your share of luck, but you wanted two shares. Now you're as poor as me who was born with no luck at all, except my health and strength. But at least I've got friends. Don't despair, poor dragon, as your go-between I'm determined to bring you two twins back together. I believe the luck in your grandma's coins will return if you two make it up. By the way, what happened to the lucky coins? I suppose you spent them being the criminal that you are?"

Then an amazing thing happened. Opening wide his mouth the poor dragon lolled out his tongue. Balanced on the twin forks were two common copper coins, still bright despite the passing of the centuries. The dragon allowed them to chink to the ground where they lay shining on the cold grey gravel.

"Since the day I ran away I've kept them under my tongue for safety," said the shamed dragon. "Hoping and praying that they would bring me the luck and the fame I craved."

"But knowing deep down that they never would," said Eric, patting the poor creature's orange neck. "Never mind, there's always hope. Dry those tears, foolish dragon. While my sheep are safely grazing you and I are going down the mountain to confront your rich brother. Come on, slide off that pile of earth and gravel and follow me. And don't look so frightened and glum. I'll coach you on what you need to say to your twin as we journey down."

And slipping the lucky coins into his pouch, Eric crooked the reluctant dragon around the neck and led him at a fast lumbering back down the mountain . . .

"Hello, rich dragon, hold your fire . . ."
Eric shouted through his cupped hands as they
neared the cave. "Guess who I'm bringing to see
you . . ."

The rich dragon looked up from counting
his treasures for the millionth time. Seeing his
long-gone twin standing forlornly behind Eric
his hatred boiled over. Bouts of flames bellowed
from his nostrils as he sought to destroy the
brother he had hated for so long. Death was
prevented by a simple shepherd boy who
marched bravely into the flames, his sheepskin
hat on fire. Shielding his face from the heat, Eric
smacked the rich dragon on the nose, at the
same time crooking the poor dragon forward.

"Stop it, you stupid dragon," he cried. "Your
twin has something to say. Let him speak before
you burn us both to ashes. Give him a chance to
make amends for the terrible wrong he did all
those thousands of years ago. Or have you lost
the skill of listening after all those centuries
alone?"

The rich dragon drew back, his eyes filled
with tears of love and hate, such was his
confusion. Obeying Eric's crook the poor

dragon crept forward, his head humbly bowed.

"Dear brother," he said, brokenly. "I've come down the mountain on bended knee to beg your forgiveness for stealing your lucky coin when we were small. I can only say that my crime has never brought me luck, but only misery. The magic in grandma's coins turned to evil when I committed that terrible theft. I have always been as poor as the poorest church mouse, and much more lonely."

"He's telling the truth, honest," said Eric, nodding his singed head. "I saw inside his cave and there was nothing of value just dirt and grit. I can also vouch for how sorry he is. He wept buckets of tears down the back of my scorched tunic whilst lumbering down the mountain. So, can't you two lonely dragons make your peace? Can't you stop hating each other when all you want is to be together?"

"How can I forgive him?" sobbed the rich dragon. "Can you imagine waking up to the voice of your grandma shrieking that your twin brother is a no-good thief who will spend the lucky coins on fast living. Now can you understand, shepherd boy, why I hate to look my brother in the face?"

"But I didn't spend the lucky coins on bad living," cried the poor dragon.

"And I can prove it," said Eric. Reaching into his scorched pouch he drew out the lucky copper coins and flourished them triumphantly. "You see, rich dragon, here are your grandma's coins. Your twin brother never spent a cent of them. They've been safe under his tongue for the last ten thousand years. Now call him a fast living nere-do-well"

"The lucky coins . . . grandma's lucky coins . . ." gabbled the rich dragon, snatching them from Eric's hand and stuffing them into his mouth.

"Hey, now who's the thief?" protested the poor dragon. "One of those coins belongs to me."

"Let your brother express his joy," said Eric, sternly. "You've been rolling those coins around your mouth for centuries, allow your twin to roll them round for a few moments at least. Try to control your selfish nature, poor dragon."

Because of the scorching he had endured that day, Eric perched very gingerly on a rock to watch and smile as the dragons gradually got to know each other and become loving brothers again. Feeling a bit out of it, Eric began to feel a mite lonely as shepherd boys do when they haven't got much to think about. So he was pleased when the lamb who was born to stray came gambolling down the mountain to bury its head in his crook. Then suddenly the dragons stopped laughing and bellowing and hugging each other. They went into a whispering huddle, glancing at Eric from time to time. Fearing the worst the boy steeled himself for a roasting as the rich dragon approached, his orange face serious.

"Scruffy shepherd boy," he said, "my twin and I cannot express in words the thanks we owe you for bringing us together."

"Thank you very much," said Eric, relieved. "But there's really no need to express anything. To see you both smiling and happy is enough."

"So," continued the dragon, gravely, "we are going to show our gratitude another way."

"That's very thoughtful," said Eric, brightening. "I'd be pleased if you'd give me a tiny speck of treasure to buy a new pair of breeches and a tunic. You and your twin have scorched these beyond repair."

At this both dragons began to roar with laughter, much to Eric's disappointment. He believed he at least deserved a little something for bringing the twins back together.

"You don't understand," chuckled the rich dragon, seeing Eric's face. "My twin and I have all the luck and treasure we need just being united again. We have no use for hoards of gold and gems any more. So we've decided to give it all to you, ragged shepherd boy, for you look like you need some of your own."

"What, the whole heap of it?" asked Eric amazed.

"Every last speck," cried both dragons, happily. "We brothers have the lucky coins our grandma willed us, we want for nothing more."

"I don't know what to say," said Eric, quite overcome. "Except to thank you very much again, though I don't know what I'll spend it on . . ."

But he did, for Eric thought a lot as shepherd boys do. He also seemed quite prepared to have wealth beyond his wildest dreams. Putting two fingers in his mouth he gave a shrill whistle. As if to a plan, four strapping sheep came trotting down the mountain wearing empty, grass-woven panniers. Had Eric already worked out the outcome of uniting the dragons, that because of their new-found love they would scorn wealth and give it all away? Or had he saddled up his sheep in hope? Eric wasn't saying and the happy dragons didn't ask. Soon the boy was busily loading the panniers with the glittering treasure. When every last diamond and gold coin was packed he turned and hugged the grinning dragons.

"Thank you, and may you enjoy bellowing at each other for the next ten thousand years," he said, sincerely. "And I promise to come and see my two best friends as often as possible."

"If you don't we'll bellow the mountains down," joked the dragons, waving a tearful goodbye as Eric drove his sheep back down the mountain to his village in the lowlands.

Eric's family and the villagers had to shield their eyes against the dazzle as the panniers were unpacked. They were astonished to hear that the treasure was a gift from two orange dragons. In the stories they had been told as children, dragons greedily hoarded treasure and never gave a speck away. But they believed their singed shepherd boy, for he wasn't one to lie. So when he made a promise to the villagers that astonishing day, they knew it would soon come true.

First of all Eric built a nice roomy house for his family. Then he built smart roomy houses for the villagers who mostly lived in poor hovels. Then marshalling every cart in the village he took his family and neighbours to the city market. Delving into a sack brimming with gold and jewels he generously paid for everything the poor villagers had long desired. For his own family he bought a pony and trap for his mother and sisters so they could trot into town for the latest flowery dresses and ribbons. He didn't forget his old father who had stayed behind in the village. For him he bought a new pipe and baccy, plus a silver-topped cane to hobble on when his shooting pains were bad. For himself he bought a new suit of sheepskin breeches, his old clothes being scorched beyond repair.

Then it was home in merry procession back to the village, the lowing of the milking cows and the grunting of the fat pigs and the clucking and honking of the hens and geese almost drowning out the happy song of the villagers.

Eric did not forget the poor parish priest. Heaping his collection plate with rubies and pearls, soon the delighted man was able to build a solid stone church with a steeple, crowned by a golden weathercock. Then Eric looked around for other good causes to spend his treasure on, for he was a kind lad and liked to help everyone.

Yet as he basked in wealth and fame he felt there was something missing from his life. Something he was in danger of forgetting. It was the clear fresh loneliness of the moutains where once a shepherd boy could commune with nature and his quiet thoughts. It was the wayward lamb, the constant stray, who made up Eric's mind. Gambolling from the flock it nudged at the boy's crook that leaned unused against the wall. And as if on cue came a sad bellowing from high up the mountain.

"I'm coming, dragons," he yelled back at the hills. "And no fire breathing, for I'll be wearing my brand new suit of clothes."

And crooking his restless flock together, Eric went back to the shepherding he so loved and missed, eager to munch his bread and cheese in thoughtful silence, and anxious to see his beloved dragon friends again. And as he steadily climbed into the hills he felt that beautiful sense of peace again, a peace that no amount of wealth could buy.

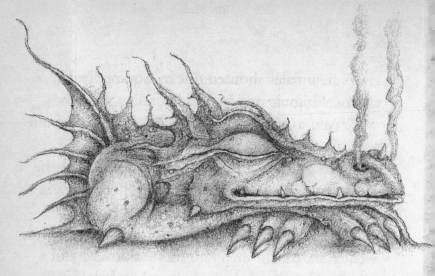

# GOBBINS

England looked set to be a wonderful place under the new reign of Good King Alf. After his coronation in London he began to scrap many unfair laws, adding just one new one. Then he sent out his messengers to spread the news throughout his kingdom, for he loved to keep in touch with his subjects, being the first good king in ages.

In the tiny hamlet of Dragonswood the people gathered on Goose Green to hear the king's new rules shouted out by Squire Groat, the local bigwig and bighead.

"From Good King Alf, greetings to our beloved subjects," bellowed Squire Groat, reading from a crackly parchment. "Your loyal love makes us very humble. God bless you all."

"Fancy Good King Alf bothering to greet and bless us," whispered Peg to her brother Will as they craned to see above the crowd.

"That's because he's a caring king," said Will. "Not like his father King Bert the Horrible who was overthrown for chopping too many heads off."

"But why is King Alf called 'Good' already?" said Peg, puzzled. "He was only crowned when the buds came out in May."

"Hush," hissed the people with fat purses, "we're trying to hear about the lenient tax laws"

The tax laws were lenient indeed. Squire Groat was beaming as he bawled them out.

"Well he would, wouldn't he," sniffed Peg. "Beam, I mean. Considering that Squire Groat owns nearly every scrap of land in the shire."

"Be quiet," hissed the poor people. "We need to know what Good King Alf is going to do about poverty."

The king's poor law was more than fair. The
parchment read . . . 'that from this day we banish
poverty from our realm forever . . .' which
brought lusty cheers from the ragged and hungry
who had been praying that their new king would
not let them down. Squire Groat continued to
bellow out more laws, each one sounding better
than the last for somebody in the crowd.

"What a very kind king," said Peg,
astonished. "I believe he's drawn up a lovely law
for everyone to be pleased with."

"We won't tell you again," growled the
grown-ups. "Goose Green is no place for
children when important laws are being read out.
We know who you are. You're those impudent
Crackling kids who should be home in the forest,
helping Mrs Crackling to milk the goats and
gather the firewood. So, why aren't you home
being a help to your mother?"

"Because even children are entitled to hear
the king's law," retorted Will. "Anyway we did
our chores early this morning, and mum was
very pleased."

"My daughter is at home learning her sewing
stitches," snapped the fat man with a purse to
match, glaring at Peg.

"And there are some daughters who hate sewing," glared Peg.

The wealthy gentleman was just about to clip Peg's ear when Squire Groat began to boom out more astonishing laws.

It was becoming clear that Good King Alf was trying to be popular by being very caring as his laws got kinder and kinder. Two laws especially pleased Will and Peg. The first read . . . 'that from this day we allow all hobbling and crackling crones to stir bat wings and toad livers in black cauldrons . . . to also own black cats with evil eyes . . . to fly around on broomsticks without the fear of being burned at the stake as a witch . . . for grandmas weren't born to be perfect."

"That sounds just like ours," said Peg, nudging Will. "Never again will we have to bundle grandma Crackling into the cupboard when the soldiers rap on our door with their swords. Now she can stir the most horrible things and pour them down our throats in the legal name of Good King Alf."

"So long as she doesn't stir any more boil potion," winced Will. "I couldn't sit down for a week after she smeared that on."

"Be quiet!" shouted the landowners and the poachers. "We're trying to hear about the new game-laws."

"Concerning the game-laws," trumpeted Squire Groat. Then his beam faded to a frown. It was obvious he hated having to read them out. But he did just in case the king didn't feel good all the time and ordered his head to be chopped off. Concealing his anger he read from the parchment . . .

". . . furthermore, we Good King Alf declare that if a poor man shoots a deer in the forest he will no longer be hung, drawn and quartered if caught. For even the lowliest of my subjects are entitled to a good supper."

"That law will make dad's day," grinned Will. "And mine. I'm sick of dormouse and boiled cabbage."

"And I detest baked hedgehog and carrots," shuddered Peg. "It's about time we all enjoyed a nice bit of venison."

But when a new king drafts laws there is always one law that upsets someone. For Will and Peg it was the last law at the end of the scroll. Squire Groat had a look of triumph on his face as he read it out, his fat finger wagging accusingly at the two children . . .

" . . . but finally, we Good King Alf must end with a stern law. From this day we banish all dragons from our kingdom. As a concerned king I will not allow fire-breathing, gold-hoarding, damsel-ransoming pagan creatures in my realm. Any person harbouring a dragon, or even telling a dragon story will be hung, drawn and quartered in their local Goose Green. A long time ago when I was a hostage prince in my horrible father's dungeon a dragon appeared in a blaze of light and promised that I would be king before the next new full moon. Trembling and waiting with hope in my heart, sadly I say that it was ten full moons before I was proclaimed Good King Alf. Therefore I banish all untrust-worthy dragons from the land."

"I'm beginning to wish King Bert The Horrible was still on the throne," yelled Will, outraged. "At least he didn't persecute dragons."

"After all, dragons can be as late as anyone," shouted Peg. "Perhaps the rescuing dragon went to the wrong castle by mistake. Even dragons can be confused when kings own castles all over the place."

"Be warned, young Crackling brats, we

know your secret," said Squire Groat with satisfaction. Then, with saintly gestures, he rounded off the speech of the new king . . . "And so, my loyal subjects, let us fall to our knees and thank Him for sending you a new and caring king . . . amen."

Squire Groat was the first to rise from his fat knees. He hurried away to prowl his lands for poachers who might already be using his deer for hunting practice. He was a worried squire indeed as he raced panting and belly-bobbling through the copses and dells of his property.

The last to leave Goose Green were Will and Peg. Shocked and shaken by the king's dragons law, they went home with dragging feet to their humble cottage, deep in the thick green forest.

Pushing open the door a familiar scene awaited them. At the rough-hewn table sat father Crackling, smiling at some memory as he whittled a new leg for an old stool. At the fire busied mother Crackling, sniffing and tasting the hedgehog and cabbage stew bubbling in her pot. On one side of the hearth crouched granny Crackling, cackling creepy rhymes as she crumbled herbs and dried frogs eyes between her gnarly fingers. On the other side of the hearth sprawled the family pet, Gobbins, his yellow eyes intent on the pictures he saw in the glowing fire. Now and then he would flick out his tongue to collect the dead ashes from the grate, they being his favourite snack.

Gobbins was blue and green in a spotted way, but the family rarely noticed. He reeked of magic and mysterious things, but no-one thought it strange. Often he would puff out a slim jet of flame to down a troublesome bluebottle. The family thought this quite reasonable. Crisped or swatted, everybody hated bluebottles. Gobbins hated exercise. He would roll his yellow eyes when the children tied his rope-lead around his neck. But he was always good-natured as he shambled between them for his weekly stroll through the forest. In short, Gobbins was the nicest, most beloved pet in the world. He was also very useful. He was the perfect set of puffing bellows when mother Crackling needed her fire to glow. The problem was that Gobbins was now illegal. For Gobbins was a dragon, and that was the rub as children entered their cottage, Will grim-faced, Peg in floods of tears.

"Whatever's the matter?" said their parents, concerned. "Were the new king's laws so very bad?"

Putting an arm around his sister, Will recited Good King Alf's laws. About how poor people were no longer allowed to be poor, and how everyone should have a nice bit of venison in their supper pots, and how witches would no longer be burned at the stake for mixing potions. That law brought a cackle of merriment from Grandma Crackling, her single tooth waggling in its socket. On her shoulder her green-eyed cat yowled his approval.

"But they sound like very good laws," said father puzzled.

"You haven't heard the last law of all," wept Peg. "You tell them, Will."

"Yes, a very terrible law," said Will, bitterly. "It seems that Good King Alf hates dragons. Everyone who owns one is ordered to turn it in for execution. If the owners of the dragon do not obey they'll be hung, drawn and quartered. Which means that the life of our pet is hanging by a thread."

"What, our Gobbins' life hanging by a thread?" said mother, shocked. "What would I do with the empty space in my hearth if they dragged him away? Who would keep the blue-bottles from buzzing round my table? And who would bellow my fire into a hot glow?"

"But surely Gobbins is no threat to the king," said father, angrily. "He wouldn't harm a fly, except for bluebottles."

"The king doesn't know that," sobbed Peg, burying her face in her mother's greasy apron. "What will we do when Squire Groat and his men come for him?"

"Just let that fat Squire lay one finger on Gobbins," growled father, hugging Peg to his rough woodcutter's jerkin.

"He won't set foot in this cottage," cried mother Crackling, brandishing the iron poker from her fire. "Unless he wants to feel the hot end of this."

"I'll chant a spell to turn the king's bones to water," cackled grandma, spitting in the fire. "And on the night of the first full moon his ears and toes will drop off. What about Gobbins himself? He has powers enough to protect us all. His magic is strong enough to overturn all laws. But Gobbins is Gobbins and bides his time, doesn't he, my Midnight? Don't we bide our time, my lovely?"

The black cat on her shoulder yowled his agreement, his green eyes blazing fire, his sharp white teeth bared.

"How could Good King Alf turn out so bad?" grieved Peg, drying her eyes on the cat's bristling fur as she stroked it.

As for Gobbins, through all the weeping and wailing and angry words he didn't so much as twitch a pointy ear but continued to gaze into the fire. Perhaps he had listened to every word. Perhaps he hadn't. Perhaps he really was a dragon of wondrous powers, perhaps he wasn't. Perhaps he could save himself and his family from the chop, who knew he couldn't? But one thing was clear. Relaxed and gazing into the fire he seemed content to leave his fate in the hands of the Crackling family who loved him.

"We could hide Gobbins up the chimney," suggested mother. "He loves flames and smoke, so he'd come to no harm."

Will shook his head.

"Squire Groat knows that Gobbins lives here. If he and his men came searching they'd poke a spear up the chimney and bring Gobbins tumbling down. Then they'd drag him away to have his head chopped off on Goose Green."

"If that happened I'd lay my head on the block beside him," said Peg, bravely. "If I can't live with Gobbins in life, then I'll die with him in death."

"Is there no way out?" asked mother, her smoke-blackened eyes all weepy. "How can I cope without Gobbins on his hearth?"

"There is a way out," said Will, thinking. "I have a plan. When it gets dark Peg and I are going to take Gobbins for the longest walk of his life."

Gobbins rolled his yellow eyes skyward. For a non-speaking dragon he seemed to know words ever so well.

"But where will you flee with Gobbins?" asked mother, worried. "If you took him deeper into the forest Squire Groat and his men would flush him out, they being hunters."

"Gobbins won't be hidden in the forest," said Will, excitedly. "Our long walk is going to take us along The King's Highway."

"To where?" asked father.

"To London, of course," said the boy. "There to petition Good King Alf, to plead for his life. And if the three of us don't return, take heart. You can be sure we'll all face our fate with brave smiles on our faces."

"I with a red rose clasped to my breast," said Peg, romantically. "And hugging Will and Gobbins to the very end."

Granny Crackling cackled and spat into the fire again. She was kneading a lump of clay in the shape of a man with a crown on his head. Drawing some hedgehog quills from her ragged cloak she said, "Just let that king lay one harming hand on my three babies and he'll feel the sharpness of these magic quills in his backside. Unless lazy Gobbins will stir himself in time to save them all from the chop," and she cackled again, Midnight the cat spitting his fury from her shoulder.

As darkness fell the children tied the rope-lead around Gobbin's neck and coaxed him from the warm hearth out into the chilly night.

"There's a dragon moon tonight," shrieked granny, waving her broomstick at the sky. "The king will rue his wicked law if he dares to scoff at the signs."

"Please, granny, we're trying to say goodbye," said mother Crackling. On the doorstep she hugged the three travellers. "Now remember, be polite to Good King Alf and come safely home to us."

"For I'll miss your laughter," said father, awkwardly. "And your nuisance."

"And I'll miss a perfect set of bellows for my fire," said mother, turning and weeping again.

"Goodbye then," said Will and Peg, shedding tears of their own. Then, grasping Gobbin's lead, they set off through the forest towards The King's Highway, their path lit by a dragon moon . . .

Their troubles began the moment they stepped onto The King's Highway. It was Gobbins' claws. Clickerty-clack, clackerty-click, they sounded on the hard surface as he shambled along between the children.

"Please Gobbins," they hissed. "Try to walk on your heels. Squire Groat lives in the big mansion house opposite Goose Green. We'll never sneak by with you clickerty-clacking to wake the dead."

But Gobbins was hopeless at walking on his heels. Will and Peg could only pray that Squire Groat was drunk or asleep when they passed his big house.

Their hopes were in vain. Just as they were hurrying past a loud bellow halted them in their tracks. Looking up they saw Squire Groat hanging from his bedroom window wearing a long white shirt and a nightcap, and holding a bright lantern.

"Where are you taking that illegal dragon?" he bawled. "And don't say he isn't with you. I've known for a long time that you Cracklings have been hiding a dragon. Now you're trying to steal him away from the wrath of Good King Alf. Well, I'll stop your little game. I order you to tie that beast to the maypole on Goose Green so that I can chop off his head in the morning. And you can think yourselves lucky that I won't be hanging, drawing and quartering you two impudent children for breaking the law."

"You'll be all alone and fuming at that maypole in the morning," shouted Will, defiantly. "Because Peg and Gobbins and I won't be there. We're taking our Gobbins down the long road to London to appeal to the king."

"You can't appeal against the king's ruling," yelled Squire Groat.

"Oh yes we can," Peg shouted back. "We believe it's the right of every subject to argue with the king if his laws are unfair."

"There's nothing about that on my parchment," retorted the angry Squire.

"We're going to appeal to the king's heart, not to his parchment," said Will. "So I suggest you shut your window and go to bed before you catch your death of cold."

"Well," sneered the nasty man. "It'll save me a grisly task in the morning, for Good King Alf will doubtless top the three of you when you get to London. And good riddance, I say."

And on that unfeeling note he slammed his window shut.

Will and Peg felt pleased to have told Squire Groat to get off. Even their pet seemed pleased. At least he had a smile on his face as they carried on down The King's Highway, Gobbins sounding like a marching army as his claws went clickerty-clack, clackerty-click, every step of the way.

The journey to London was much further than they had thought. After just one day's march the children collapsed with blistered heels. Silently munching their bread and cheese and fitting a nosebag of cold cinders around Gobbins' neck, they slumped against a milestone. Wincing with pain they were steps away from giving up.

Then to their astonishment Gobbins awoke from his snooze and click-clacked into the road. Waggling his behind and smiling broadly, it was obvious what he had in mind. Delightedly the children climbed aboard his broad back to continue the journey in luxury, their pet's rolling motion soon soothing them to sleep the miles away.

The news of their mission had spread like wildfire. Often, when they stopped to pick blackberries from the hedgerows, nervous faces would peer at them through the leaves as other children in hiding with their own hunted dragons hissed 'good luck' before vanishing out of sight again . .

"If Good King Alf is a really good king he'll see the niceness of dragons," was the cry all the way down the long and winding road . . .

Many days later the trio were breasting the final hill before London. Will and Peg looked down and gasped. The huge city sprawled as far as the eye could see, the river Thames gliding like a silver snake through its centre. For a long time the children and Gobbins gazed at the turreted towers and the golden crosses on the church spires glinting in the morning sun.

"It's a lot grander than Dragonswood," said Will, awed. "Where do you think Good King Alf lives?"

"Probably in that tallest palace," said Peg pointing. "His home has to be tall so that his high crown doesn't bump the roof. But look, Will, there's a man with a horse and cart coming along. We can ask him."

"Pardon me, sir," said Will politely as the man reigned in his horse. The cart was heaped with fish and lobsters and ponged a lot. "Could you tell us if Good King Alf lives in that very tall palace?"

"You mean Westminster," grinned the fisherman. He crossed himself. "He does, and may The Lord see the goodness in him."

"It says in his parchment of laws that he hates dragons," said Will. "He hates them so much that he's ordered all their heads to be chopped off. I can't see much goodness in that, master fisherman."

"Dragons are the salt of the earth," said Peg, hugging Gobbins who was having another snooze.

"I agree," smiled the fisherman, glancing down. "I had a dragon myself when I was your age. Wonderful company, he was. Wouldn't hurt a fly, except bluebottles."

"Which is why we have travelled all the way from Dragonswood," explained Peg. "We are here to plead for the life of Gobbins, in fact, for the life of every dragon in the land. We're sure that when Good King Alf sees how nice our pet is he'll strike the unfair law from his parchment. If he doesn't, Will and I are going to demand that we are hung, drawn and quartered beside our Gobbins."

"I pray it doesn't come to that, little travellers," said the nice fisherman. "But come, climb on my cart and I'll set you down at the foot of the king's grand steps. If a cat can look at a king, surely a nice dragon can."

The children coaxed Gobbins aboard the cart, eagerly scrambling up beside him. Wallowing amongst the fish and lobsters, Gobbins didn't smile once throughout the journey down to the city. The reason was simple. Dragons hate the smell of fish. He didn't complain, for dragons never do. But he did begin to smile again when he and the children climbed from the cart to stand before a soar of magnificent marble steps.

"I'll give you a bit of advice that might help

your cause," said the fisherman. "It's not much, but the king has a sickly son, Prince Fred. Win the smile of the prince and you might win the good heart of the king. And now, farewell and good luck, small law-breakers."

"Thank you, master fisherman," said Will and Peg, sad to see him go. "And may the emory of your own childhood dragon stay with you forevermore. And may you sell every one of your fishes and lobsters . . ."

And their friend was gone, the cart hauled away by the lovely brown horse into the bustling, shouting market-place and the depths of the city.

"I'm frightened, Will," whispered Peg, glancing up. "These steps are made for giants."

"We're together, the three of us," said Will, squeezing her hand. "We must be brave, even if our lives end here. Remember, Peg, we'll never slink back to Dragonswood without a pardon for Gobbins."

"The death of Gobbins will mean the death of all three," vowed Peg. "So, Will, let us march upwards and bravely face our fate."

Both children were hesitant to set a first foot on the marble steps, but the problem was solved for them. Once an obedient follower, Gobbins now led. Up the steps he clickerty-clacked pulling the children on the rope-lead behind him. Now he was smiling more warmly than he had ever smiled. In fact his smile was so melting that the guards at the top of the steps fell in love with him and, forgetting their orders, allowed the three to enter through the huge doors into the Great Hall of Westminster. But then some of the guards had children who also owned illegal dragons.

Inside the hall and awed by its splendour, the children were unsure of what to do next.

"Where do you think a king would live in such a magnificent palace?" whispered Will to Peg. "He must have a hundred rooms to choose from."

"A king would live in a throne room," said sensible Peg. "But here comes a pretty man, he'll tell us where to find Good King Alf."

The man who confronted them was certainly gorgeously dressed in his red velvet cloak and his weasel-skin hat with feathers, but his face was angry. He stood haughtily barring their way, holding his long thin nose with a scented scrap of lace.

"Who allowed you into the royal palace?" he demanded. "How dare common urchins invade the privacy of the king smelling of fish? And with an outlaw dragon if my eyes don't deceive me."

"We are Will and Peg Crackling from Dragonswood," said Will, defiantly. "And this outlaw is Gobbins Crackling. We have come to confront our king about his unfair dragon law."

"Anyway, who are you in your silly hat?" snapped Peg, her courage back. "I wouldn't wear a silly thing like that even in a Goose Green Passion Play."

"I am Lord Gushing of Creeping Castle," answered the outraged courtier. "And no one sees His Majesty except through me. And I'll have you know that this hat cost me a fortune in Groats, you impudent wench. But enough of this . . . guards . . . guards . . ."

The guards came rushing. Once their faces had smiled, now they were white with fear.

"Bind this outlaw in chains!" thundered Lord Gushing. "And tie the hands of these impudent whelps. Then hurl them into the king's throne room to grovel before our good and wise law maker."

The terrified guards obeyed. Bound and bewildered the three were dragged across the hall to another set of heavy doors. Creaking them open the guards flung their prisoners inside. The floor of the throne room was so slippery that Will and Peg slithered the whole of its length on their stomachs, Gobbins in his clanking chains rolling over and over beside them. They came to a stop with a bump against what appeared to be a raised stage. The frightened children looked up. Over them loomed the hateful figure of Lord Gushing, evily kicking Gobbins as he sprawled so helplessly there.

"All rise for Good King Alf and Prince Fred," boomed a voice. There was the sound of boots shuffling and swords clanking in the echoing throne room.

Craning their heads the children saw through their tears a tall man entering the throne room wearing a very high crown. Very regally he sat down on a golden throne that was placed stage-centre. In his lap he cradled a small boy. The face of the child was pinched and blue as it coughed and wheezed in a pitiful way. Pathetically the sickly Prince Fred wore a small crown on his head that kept slipping lopsidedly each time he coughed and wailed.

"Good morning to our Noble Lord and his merry Prince Fred," fawned Lord Gushing, bowing low. "At your mighty feet lie three prisoners caught by my own hand while trying to sneak into your palace. As you'll note, Sire, they are two common urchins and a dragon banned by your own strict law. I trust you'll wish to scathe them with your royal tongue before I have them dragged away to the block and the scaffold? To set an example to others who would flout your mighty power?"

Good King Alf looked keenly down at Will and Peg. Then he looked at Gobbins snuffling and choking in his chains. Then he glanced at the distressed child in his lap. Something inside him stirred, for he said, "Let the children speak. Let them defend their dragon. For all of my subjects are entitled to petition their king. Free them from their bonds."

Lord Gushing was scarlet with rage as he cut the children free with a little jewelled dagger. But he kept his face averted lest the king should see the unfair hatred he bore for ordinary children who didn't live in castles. On the other hand the hearts of Will and Peg were filled with hope as they rubbed their sore wrists and climbed to kneel humbly before Good King Alf and his poor whooping, coughing son. Peg took extra heart to notice that the king had the nicest, kindest brown eyes she had ever seen. She nudged Will to speak, to put the case for their pet lying helpless in his chains.

"Good King Alf," said the boy, finding his voice. "We have travelled all the way from Dragonswood to complain about the last law in your parchment. While the laws before are good, the last one is very bad."

"And we are prepared to die if you don't tear that law to tatters," cried Peg, rising from her knees and pointing down at Gobbins. "Chop off his head and you can chop off mine."

"You dare defy my dragon law?" said the King, his brown eyes kind, a smile on his regal lips. "Give me your reason, little subjects."

"Just because you had a bad experience with a dragon doesn't mean that all dragons are bad," said Will. "On our way from Dragonswood lots of children and their dragons were cheering us every step of the way."

"Even the fisherman who brought us here to your palace had a dragon when he was small," said Peg. "And that lovely man has only fond memories of him."

"So, even the sellers of fish in my realm question my laws," said the King. "Tell me why my subjects love dragons so?"

"For a start they are perfect walking companions when they aren't dragging behind on their leads," said Peg. "And if the cooking fire is dying they are experts at bellowing it into life again."

"Also a dragon is proof against a bluebottle in your soup," said Will. "And no pet smiles more than a dragon when their owners are down in the dumps."

"Like Prince Fred your son," said Peg. "Pardon me Sir, but I think that poor lad would benefit in health if he had a dragon of his own. I'm sure he wouldn't whoop and cough so much if he had a smiling pet like Gobbins."

"You try to pull the wool over the eyes of His Majesty with lies?" cried the odious Lord Gushing. "Prince Fred is attended by the best doctors in the land. And you dare to say that the smile of a dragon is more effective than purges and leeches? My King, allow me to execute these three immediately."

"Wait!" commanded the King. "Release the dragon. Let him work his magic smile upon my son, if he can. But be warned, small children, if your Gobbins proves to be a fraud I will lawfully order him to the chopping block."

Gobbins was unbound from his chains. Cramped with pain he slowly got to his clawed feet, stretching and flicking his long tail, his yellow eyes blinking in the light from the smoky torches that illuminated the throne room. At that moment Will and Peg were praying that granny Crackling was right and that their pet was much more than a lazy hearth dragon. Please, grant us just a smidgen of magic, was their prayer.

There was total silence in the hall as the king leant from his throne and held out his sickly son. Gobbins advanced, his beautiful-ugly head almost touching the boy. And Gobbins smiled the sweetest smile the world had ever seen as he flicked out his long tongue and gently licked that poor, pinched face. And all at once Prince Fred was healthily-pink and kicking, his delighted chuckles ringing round the throne room amid the gasps of astonishment from the nobles gathered there. For all had witnessed a miracle, or a touch of loving, dragon magic. For every child knew that dragons love children.

The kind brown eyes of Good King Alf were
filled with tears as he rose from his throne with
his drawn sword. Will and Peg were filled with
alarm as he brought down the blade on Gobbins.
But their fears were unfounded.

"Arise, Sir Gobbins of Dragonswood," said
the king. Then he raised his voice so that all
should hear his words. "And from this day We,
Good King Alf, do tear the unfair dragon law
from our parchment. From this day my healed
son Prince Fred will have a dragon of his own to
love and take for walks. We have spoken . . ."

And then he chucked Will and Peg under their chins, ordering the fuming Lord Gushing that the three be honoured with a royal escort all the way back to Dragonswood.

It was truly like a royal procession as the children and Gobbins were borne back along the King's Highway towards home. The news had spread far and wide. Children no longer lurked in the hedgerows with their dragons as the colourful party passed, Gobbins wearing a golden sash around his blue and green spotted shoulders, smiling broader than ever.

"Hurrah for Sir Gobbins of Dragonswood and the Crackling children!" was the cry. "Who cares if they stink of fish. Now we can come out of the cupboard and fill Merry England with all the dragons it deserves."

"I can't wait to see Squire Groat's face," said Peg with a giggle as they neared Goose Green.

"Make way for a knight in the realm!" bawled the captain of the escort as the pompous squire tried to bar their way with bluster. Because he was drunk the news hadn't reached him.

"What knight?" shouted Squire Groat. "All I see is an illegal dragon coming back under escort to have his head chopped off on Goose Green."

"You'd chop off the head of Sir Gobbins of Dragonswood?" said the stern captain of the escort. "Beware I don't chop off yours. This dragon and these children are under the protection of Good King Alf. Get out of the way or suffer the wrath of the king."

"Unless you want the King to fine you and your rich purse, Squire Groat!" shouted Peg. "Never think of coming to poke your nose up our chimney for dragons again."

"And may all your candles on your rich table blow out," said Will. "Because you've spent your life snuffing out the candles of others."

Squire Groat was a broken man as he tottered to slump beneath the maypole on Goose Green. When they weren't cheering the triumphant return of the trio the people of Dragonswood were jeering him for the way he had treated them for so many years. There was only one soul with compassion for a pompous, now deflated man. Gobbins paused in his progress to clickerty-clack from the road, lick the tip of the man's red nose, because, who knows, perhaps even a wicked man can be healed by the forgiving love of a dragon . . .

Will and Peg burst open the door of the cottage deep in the forest. They had so much to say, so much excitement bursting to come out. But they couldn't find the words as their home was as blessedly, peacefully calm as it had ever been. Father was sitting and smiling and fitting a second new leg on an old stool, mother was bending over her pot of bubbling venison stew, whilst grandma Crackling cackled as ever in her secret world, her scary cat yowling on her shoulder. For some time the children stood there, words forgot, just glad to be home. Gobbins made the first move. With a wide smile he ambled to fill the empty space beside the hearth. Sighing he slumped back into his beloved role of a lazy hearth-dragon, glad to puff mother's dying fire into a bright flame again.

"Mum . . . dad . . ." said Peg, at last. "Do you know the king has torn the unfair dragon law from his parchment, all because of Gobbins?"

"I'm not surprised, dear," said her mother.

"And would you believe that our pet is now Sir Gobbins of Dragonswood?" said Will to his dad.

"About time too," smiled the wood-carving man. "But nobleness runs in our family."

"And magic," screeched granny, cackling with laughter and digging the smiling Gobbins in the ribs.

"And love," said Will and Peg, sitting down to the rough-hewn table to enjoy a steaming bowl of venison stew.

And it was a lovely full moon in the forest that night. The same moon that was shining on a happy king and his happy son.

Good night.

# MISS
# PARSON'S
## PET

Little Joe Bloggs lived under a hill overlooking the school. Every morning he gazed out of his turf spy hole and watched the children trooping through the gates to tackle their lessons. Little Joe was in love with the idea of going to school. He yearned to wear a school scarf and carry a satchel bulging with books. He was certain he would be clever at lessons and brilliant at sport if only he could be a real pupil. He blurted out his hopes and dreams to his parents.

"You wouldn't fit in," warned his father. "Our sort have never been welcome in human society."

"Nonsense," said mother. "Our Little Joe is as good as any child. I say we enrol him for the next term. We'll soon get him a proper coloured scarf and a satchel. And we've got plenty of dusty books on our shelves to make him look business-like. Why should our son have to hide himself away just because he looks a bit different?"

"Very well," sighed father. "But I can see trouble ahead."

Little Joe beamed his beautiful smile. At last his dream was about to come true. In his mind he was already top of the class in everything.

"Remember, Little Joe," said his mother. "When joining a school one must always show respect by taking the teacher a small gift. And one must always wear a smile even though things are going badly. You can always weep your heart out when you get home, if you have to."

"Also very important," said his worried father. "Never be late for your first day at school."

But because of the enormous weight of his satchel, Little Joe was . . .

The children were back after the long summer break. There was lots of jostling and excited talk in the corridor as friends swapped holiday snaps and compared suntans. There was also much nudging and glancing at the shy newcomers who were pretending not to be new at all. Suddenly there was a hush as Miss Parsons came striding down the corridor, her arms piled high with papers and books. The old dragon had arrived to spoil everyone's day.

"No gathering in herds," she snapped, unlocking the classroom door. "File inside and sit down quietly."

There were twenty desks in the classroom. After some quarrelling and chair-leg scraping, nineteen were filled. In the meantime Miss Parsons had arranged herself at her high desk.

"The register," she said, opening her ledger and unscrewing the top from her fountain-pen. "Starting at the front, call out your names and addresses in a clear voice. And there will be no giggling. There is nothing amusing about a name and address. First . . ."

"John Wayne Brown," said the boy blushing. "Number seven, Poplar Road. But they call me Jack, Miss Parsons."

The class stifled their giggles as Miss Parsons entered the details in her book. "And the next?"

"Madonna Monroe," said Maddy, biting her lip. "Number twenty one, Elmtree Avenue. But . . ."

"I'm not here to enter 'buts' in my register." said Miss Parsons, glaring. She carried on around the class until everyone was entered and blotted. She was just about to slam her book shut when she noticed something. Taking off her glasses she polished them and peered again. She began to look very annoyed. It was just as well the cane had been banned from the school."

"We have a joker," she snapped. "There are twenty desks in my classroom and only nineteen names in my register."

"That's because one of the desks is empty, Miss Parsons," said Jack, turning to point. "The desk at the back by the door. The desk nobody wants."

Just then the door squeaked open and in shuffled the missing pupil. Around his neck he wore a brand new school scarf, and he was lugging the heaviest satchel any child had ever seen. He bore no trace of suntan. This was because he was bright orange from the top of his

crested head to the tip of his long curling tail.
His toe-nails were enormously long which was
probably why he wasn't wearing ordinary trainers
like everyone else.

Watched by the astonished children he
waddled down the aisle between the desks to
Miss Parson's high perch. Dipping an orange claw
into his satchel he produced a rosy-red apple
which he placed on the teacher's blotting pad.
Then beaming all over his orange face he
lumbered back to squeeze his fat body into the
seat behind the empty desk, wrapping his long
tail around his midriff.

"Are we dreaming?" asked Jack in a whisper.

If Jack was dreaming the orange pupil
certainly wasn't. Again his claw delved into his
bulging satchel. His cleverness shrieked out to
every child in the class as he stacked *The Complete
Works of Shakespeare* on his desk. Then he leaned
back in his seat and gazed adoringly at Miss
Parsons, as if eager to be taught something he
didn't already know.

"I was just about to close my register," said
Miss Parsons. But her eyes were kind behind her
spectacles. "Just don't be late again. And now call
out your name and address."

"Little Joe Bloggs," said the latecomer in a clear voice. "From under the hill at the back of the school."

"Thank Heavens for a good plain name," murmured Miss Parsons as she wrote the facts down and blotted them.

"But Miss Parsons," shouted Maddy, springing to her feet. "You've just entered a dragon in your register. He isn't a proper child like us. His Shakespeare books speak volumes. No ordinary pupil can quote *Hamlet* and be bright orange at the same time. If Little Joe Bloggs isn't a dragon pretending to be a child then me and the class don't know nothing."

"Certainly not grammar," winced Miss Parsons. "I despair for your future, Madonna Monroe. I hope you do better in English this term for the sake of your job prospects."

Madonna pouted and sat down.

Little Joe was still beaming but looking a bit puzzled. He had been expecting his schooldays to be the happiest days of his life. He had hoped to be firm friends with all his schoolmates by now. So where was all the ragging and joking he was longing to be part of? His lovely smile faltered as another pupil stood up to say more nasty things.

"Miss Parsons," said Jack. "We children are simply saying that little Joe Bloggs doesn't fit into our school. No genuine child would come to school with an apple for the teacher. He may be a creep and a Shakespeare genius, but he'll always be an orange dragon to us.

"Silence!" ordered Miss Parsons. "I will not have jealousy and name-calling in my classroom. Little Joe is now in my register which means he is entitled to a superior education. A dragon indeed. Little Joe Bloggs is a bright little boy who's come to school to learn like anyone else. And there's a lesson for you all. For it's pupils like him who get dozens of A-levels and go on to row the boat for Oxford. Now, I insist that you all turn around in your seats and apologise to him for your rudeness and bad manners."

As she spoke the truth dawned on the children. While they saw an orange dragon beaming behind a pile of clever books, Miss Parsons saw only a polite and eager pupil who was going to put everyone else at the bottom of the class. They howled with disbelief and envy, but their teacher was unmoved. Pointing her pen at the loudest protesters she warned, "Do as I say unless you want to be sent home with Black

Spot letters to show your parents."

The threat of the dreaded Black Spot letter quelled all but the bravest heart. The cowed children turned around in their seats and chorused, "We apologise for calling you a creepy orange dragon, Little Joe . . ."

Little Joe's lumpy face creased into a joyful grin. At last he felt a friend amongst friends. He began planning the first practical joke he would play in the playground. Then . . .

"Even though I'm forced to apologise, he's still an ugly orange dragon," shouted a defiant lad. "You wait till we get you at playtime, Bloggsy."

"Nor will I tolerate bullying, Elvis Johnson," snapped Miss Parsons. Swiftly she scrawled a fountain-pen letter and sealed it in an envelope. Then, watched by every eye, she licked and stuck on a terrible Black Spot. With a crooking finger she beckoned Elvis to her desk. "You are banned from school for the rest of the day. Take this letter home for your parents to read. And when you report back in the morning I want to see one hundred neatly written lines that read, 'I must not call my classmate an ugly orange dragon', and take off that insolent cap when you approach my desk."

Elvis pulled off his beloved baseball cap and slouched to Miss Parson's desk. Stuffing the Black Spot letter into his back pocket he shambled from the room, slamming the door behind him. During the shocked silence that followed, Little Joe made another terrible mistake. He began to clap and cheer and beam even wider. In his mind the class apology and the sending home of Elvis meant he was now one of the gang. He was wrong. The children began to jeer at him. They were determined that a smarmy dragon would never become one of their in-crowd . . .

"Miss Parsons!" cried Maddy. "Please give me a Black Spot letter too, because I refuse to stay in this classroom with a smirking, clapping dragon."

"That's how I feel," yelled Jack.

"We all do," shouted the angry children.

"Apart from me," said a little girl at the front. "My mum and dad will kill me if I miss a day from school. Anyway, I reckon I can beat Little Joe in the exams if I swot hard enough."

But hers was a lone voice drowned by stamping trainers and catcalls.

"Silence!" thundered Miss Parsons. "This is a place of study not a football stadium. Open your history books at page twelve. This morning we are going to discuss the Dark Ages."

"No we're not," shouted Maddy. "Because, Miss Parsons, if you don't chuck that ugly Little Joe out on his ear, we are going on strike."

"That's what I was going to say," yelled Jack.

"I'm not going on strike," said the worried little girl at the front. "I've got too much to learn and too much to lose if I step out of line."

But the rest of the children were herding behind Maddy and Jack. They were all on their feet actually challenging the stern authority of Miss Parsons.

"Very well, get out of my classroom," she stormed. "For the sensible ones who wish to stay The Dark Ages lesson will continue as normal."

Seventeen defiant children marched out of the classroom. In no time at all they were gathered in the playground waving hastily chalked banners that read:

'WHAT DO WE WANT? DRAGONS OUT. WHEN DO WE WANT IT? NOW.'

Miss Parsons ignored them. Her job was to teach obedient children, not to pacify an unruly mob. Though deep down she felt sad. Outside were so many bright pupils, capable of so much. What a pity they directed their energies into protesting against Little Joe Bloggs because of his unfortunate appearance and his eagerness to learn. For Miss Parsons refused to allow race, or creed or colour to interfere in her love for teaching. She saw a pupil and she taught. But there was one small chink in her armour. She knew that the children called her 'the old dragon' behind her back. That could have been one reason why she sided with Little Joe. But ignoring the clamour outside the classroom window she continued to do what she did best, teach, even though her class now only numbered two.

"Now, back to lessons," she said. "Who can tell me something about the time we call The Dark Ages?"

The little girl shot up her hand and began to reel off dates and the names of ledgendary kings her ambitious parents had drummed into her head.

"Very good," said Miss Parsons. Then she

turned to Little Joe who was bravely smiling through his tears in his back seat by the door. "And you, Little Joe, can you tell us a little about that dark period?"

"There were dragons in those days, Miss Parsons," said Little Joe, wiping his eyes on the back of his orange claw. "And the dragons who lived then were hated just as much as they are today."

"History is mostly sad, Little Joe," said Miss Parsons, gently. "As is the present, but hopefully not the future."

And the learning and the lessons went on in spite of the noisy crowd outside. Just before the lunch-bell rang Miss Parsons made a little speech.

"Because you've both been so attentive in spite of the noise outside, I'm going to award you each a Gold Star to put in your exercise books."

What an honour.

The two pupils looked suitably shy as she awarded them their sticky-backed stars. Then she said that as this was the first day of term it was her duty to select the Class Prefect, and her choice was Little Joe. As she gravely pinned the badge on his scarf Little Joe's delight spilled over. He beamed and punched the air with an orange fist and gave a friendly thumbs-up sign to the little girl. Alas, Little Joe had a lot to learn about the moods and tantrums of other children. They rarely smiled through their tears as he had been taught to do. For suddenly the little girl was on her feet, her eyes flashing with anger at the choice.

"I refuse to accept Little Joe as Prefect, Miss Parsons," she raged. "I need that badge much more than he does. My mum and dad wanted me to become the Class Prefect. If I go home a loser they'll make my life a misery."

"As a teacher, *I* choose the Class Prefect," said Miss Parsons, firmly. "Now, sit down at once."

"Won't," said the girl, flouncing from the classroom. "I'm going on strike with the others. I've got nothing to lose any more."

And so they were two, Miss Parsons sitting at her high desk, Little Joe sitting at the back of the room wearing a weak smile. Then the lunch bell rang.

"In spite of all that fuss lessons will resume promptly after lunch," said Miss Parsons, gathering up her books and papers and the apple and sweeping from the classroom. "And don't be late a second time Little Joe Bloggs."

The banners were stacked against the playground wall. Not even a strike was going to interfere with the serious task of playing. This was their own time, after all. As they yelled and cheered and dashed about they totally ignored Little Joe who squatted all alone eating his banana and sardine sandwiches. He yearned to play in goal between the two sweaters. He would even have enjoyed playing bounce the ball against the wall if only the girls had asked him. But they didn't. Still smiling he offered a  sandwich to anyone who came near. But this generosity was snootily refused. He was the only pupil to return to the classroom when lunch time ended. The others had picked up their banners and were striking again . . .

"Dragons out . . . dragons out . . ." they chanted outside the classroom window as Little Joe sat miserably at his desk, watching Miss Parsons chalk some numbers on her blackboard.

"This afternoon will be devoted to arithmetic," she announced, turning. "What can you tell me about the exciting mystery of numbers, Little Joe?"

But the small dragon was only concerned with one sum. That morning there had been twenty pupils. One had been sent home with a Black Spot letter leaving nineteen.

Then seventeen had walked out on strike leaving two. Finally, another had stormed out leaving one. Those were the figures the small dragon summed up in his mind. And the answer? That he was easily the most hated classmate in the world. It was no wonder he could barely smile now. Deep down Little Joe had never been mad keen to be a genius and go on to row for Oxford. He had simply been in love with the idea of going to school and having lots of friends to joke with. Now here he was all alone in the classroom with no one to throw paper darts at.

"Are you paying attention, Little Joe?" asked Miss Parsons, sharply. "Never mind gazing out of the window at that noisy crowd. Just ignore them and copy down the numbers on my blackboard into your exercise book."

But Little Joe wasn't listening. An extra wide smile was spreading across his orange face as an idea dawned. Clattering back his chair he waddled from the classroom as fast as he could.

"Where are you going?" shouted Miss Parsons. "Come back here unless you want a Black Spot letter."

Outside in the playground Jack and Maddy were sharing a banner and leading the chanting. Then to their astonishment they saw Little Joe approaching, his face determined. Parking himself in front of their banner he raised an orange claw and brandished it at the classroom window.

"WHAT DO WE WANT? DRAGONS OUT. WHEN DO WE WANT IT? NOW," he yelled at the top of his voice. Everyone fell silent, their mouths agape. Finally Jack found the words.

"What are you doing here, Little Joe?" he asked. "This strike is to get you chucked out of school. You can't demonstrate against yourself. The rules of striking don't allow it."

Everyone nodded in agreement.

"How can we chuck you out while you're trying to chuck yourself out?" argued Maddy.

Little Joe hung his head. His idea had come unstuck. He had hoped to win their hearts by supporting their cause, even if it was against himself. But you can't become one of the gang simply by joining them. You need to be accepted, and this Little Joe didn't understand, having never been to school before.

"Get back to your precious Miss Parsons, Little Joe," shouted his girl rival. "She'll soon strip you of your Class Prefect's badge when she gets hold of you. She's probably already torn the Gold Star from your exercise book. Well, she won't get mine because my book is tucked down the back of my jeans."

"Class Prefect, eh," said Jack, gazing surprised at the badge on Little Joe's scarf. "And a Gold Star winner, too. Well, well."

"And him just an ugly old dragon," scoffed the little girl.

"No he's not," snapped Maddy. She clapped her hands to her mouth when she realised what she had said.

"What does that mean?" asked Jack, curiously.

"Well, I think I like him," said Maddy, looking sheepish. "I know he's a dragon but he's beginning to be just Little Joe to me."

"And who can claim to be perfect in looks?" agreed some other children. "Some of us have knobbly knees and toes that turn in, and noses that turn up too much, but we aren't persecuted for being orange with a long tail like Little Joe. We should be striking against ourselves for being so cruel."

"That's true," said Jack. "And I must admit that Little Joe is a good sport. He's the only dragon I know who'd join in a strike against himself."

"You only know one dragon," shouted some-one. "And that's Little Joe, who deserves to be one of our gang."

"Very well," said Jack, grinning. "We'll have a vote. Hands up those who want to go back into class with Little Joe."

Eighteen beaming children shot up their hands. Including Little Joe who was voting for himself just like before. For it was being accepted that mattered, and his idea had won out. The little girl raised her hand reluctantly. But because she wasn't beaming like the rest her vote didn't count.

"Right," said Jack, smiling and bowing to Little Joe. "As our Class Prefect you must lead us back into the classroom. That way you'll get the first tongue-lashing from Miss Parsons."

"So," said Miss Parsons, glaring at them as they filed to their seats. "You've all decided to honour me with your presence again."

"It was all a mistake Miss Parsons," explained Maddy. "We realised outside that we were wrong to turn against Little Joe. Deep down he isn't an ugly dragon at all. He's just the same as us, but a different shape and colour."

"So, the strike is over, Miss Parsons," said Jack. "And we're all very sorry for disrupting your teaching."

"Disrupting your learning, you mean," corrected Miss Parsons. Then she leaned from her high desk and pointed her pen from pupil to pupil. "Today I have awarded one Black Spot, two Gold Stars and a Class Prefect's badge. I'm not going to take them back but I'm warning you all. One more squeak from any of you and I'll be writing letters and sticking Black Spots for the rest of this afternoon. Is that understood?"

"Yes, Miss Parsons," chorused the class. Little Joe's 'yes' was the happiest and loudest of all, for at last he had been accepted.

"But just in case you haven't got the message we are going to do arithmetic for the rest of the day," said the teacher. But she was smiling behind her spectacles as she said it.

The class gave a mighty groan but buckled down good-naturedly. And so started and ended the first day of school for Little Joe Bloggs who lived under the hill behind the school.

"You're late home, Little Joe," said his anxious mother. "Your banana and sardine sandwiches are curling up at the edges."

"How did it go, son?" asked his worried father. "You weren't bullied? I warned you that they don't take kindly to the likes of us."

"It's the weight of all the Shakespeare books," winced Little Joe, thumping down his satchel. Then his eyes shone as he rummaged inside. Triumphantly he produced his exercise book with its gleaming Gold Star. Then he showed them his scarf bearing the Class Prefect's badge. And to make things perfect for his father, there wasn't one sign that his son had been bullied.

"Father," said proud mother. "Not only has our Little Joe been accepted but he's won a Gold Star for excellence. And topping that, he's been made Class Prefect. I always knew we were raising a genius. He'll be rowing the boat for Oxford before we know it. Tomorrow we'll ditch the Shakespeare books and slip a few slim volumes of Plato in his satchel, instead. That should lighten the burden. But, oh father, isn't it wonderful to know that all our worries were unfounded?"

"Not quite, mum," said Little Joe. He looked almost proud as he went on. "For I haven't told you about the Black Spot letter I might be sent home with if I'm late again. Miss Parsons said, 'To be late once is annoying, to be late twice is seriously vexing, but to be late three times in a row will not be tolerated, and can only be cured by a Black Spot letter.'

"So, we'll just have to get you up earlier," said his mother, making fresh banana and sardine sandwiches.

And they did. Up at the crack of dawn was Little Joe. But he was still late for school that morning. This time it was because of the enormous stack of comics he had stuffed into his satchel to dole out to his brand new friends.

Perhaps Miss Parsons let him off one more time, perhaps she didn't. But there was no doubt that these schooldays were the happiest of times for a beaming, orange dragon called Little Joe Bloggs.

# THROUGH THE EYE
## OF THE
# DRAGON

The village of Earlswood was not a happy place. Visiting people quickly passed through as if sensing the sadness there. Rumours spread far and wide. Why were there so few children in the village? And why were the villagers so close-lipped about it? Whisper ran that strange things happened there. The whispers were right . . .

Once long ago Earlswood had been a happy place. The farmer and the priest, the blacksmith and the carpenter, all joined in with their families to celebrate at festive times of year. Until that dreadful Eastertime when they offended the King of the Dragons.

The Maypole Dance was over and The Passion Play was in full swing. Jeers and insults greeted the blacksmith as he stomped across the stage in his silly dragon costume. Loud cheers rewarded the carpenter as he advanced from the other side of the stage, his sword drawn. The play ended with the valiant hero slaying the wicked dragon to a loud applause. Then all at once the spring sky boiled with black cloud and it began to storm. Thunder rolled and lightning flashed as the villagers dashed to take cover under the porch of the church. Then to their fear and astonishment a real dragon came lumbering from the edge of the woods, his nostrils flaring, his eyes glittering with anger.

"Behold me, the King of the Dragons," he roared. "How dare you puny humans reduce me to a figure of fun."

"It was only a play, King Dragon," said the frightened priest. "It was only our blacksmith dressed in a silly costume to amuse the children. We have nothing against dragons at all. It's just

our traditional way of celebrating Eastertime. We didn't mean to offend."

"The insult remains," bellowed the dragon. "First you will apologise and then you will fall down in worship of me. That is your punishment for taking my name in vain."

"We gladly apologise for the insult to your royalty," said the carpenter. "But the people of this village will never fall down and worship you. We worship a Lord who would never rant and rage like you."

"King of the Dragons you might be, but we know our rights," cried the blacksmith. "Magna Carta was signed to protect simple folk like us against tyrants. We don't even worship King John in London anymore, let alone a fat bully like you. So be gone, unless you want to feel a tattoo on your toes from my iron hammer."

"I don't think you realise the awesome powers I possess," snapped the dragon. "I'm amazingly magical when I choose to be. I could burn your village to the ground with a single breath if I wished."

"That isn't magic, it's vandalism," scoffed a little girl from the crowd. "A real magician can pull a rabbit from his cap. So where are your rabbits when you aren't even wearing a cap?"

"I'm losing patience," warned the dragon. "I insist that you fall down on your knees before me. If you refuse, your children certainly will not. For using my powers I will spirit them away to my kingdom where they will be forced to toil as my slaves for ever."

"You can't do that," shouted the farmer, angrily. "I need my son to keep me in my old age. If it wasn't for his sweat there wouldn't be a stroke of work done on my farm. Who would pull up the parsnips, if not him?"

"And this child is the apple of my eye," cried the village seamstress, hugging her pretty daughter close. "Slavery would destroy her talent, Sir Dragon. Her only wish in life is to cut and stitch and embroider cloth for as long as her eyes last out."

"I beg you Sir King," wept the village washerwoman. "Don't snatch my girls from me. They have a huge tub of breeches and tunics to scrub at one farthing each. Spirit them away and you spirit away my poor living."

"The solution is simple," snapped the dragon. "Bow down and worship me as King of the Dragons. And here is a temptation few humans can resist. Rather than wait for your reward in Heaven, take it now," and he opened a huge paw and flung down a fistful of gold coins that rolled and clinked and glittered over the church paving stones.

The rich man of the village dashed from the crowd. So did the poorest man. They fell to their knees and began to scrabble and squabble in the mud for the larger share of the split riches, watched by many greedy eyes.

"You see, already you begin to bow to me," the dragon sneered. Then with a cruel snort from his wide nostrils he turned the gold coins to rusty dross. The rich man and the poor man slunk back into the crowd shamefaced. "Now will you do as I say? Obey me and all of your gold will stay bright. Get down on your knees and Worship the King of the Dragons, and be wealthy for evermore."

"That we cannot do," said the priest, his hands clasped together in prayer. "For we will not blaspheme the One we trust."

"Very well," raged the dragon, his eyes glowing angrily. "But be warned. One day you will hear a dragon roaring in the woods. That day will be the beginning of much weeping for you stubborn people," and turning he shambled back into the woods, the trees on either side bursting into flames from his angry breath.

As the days passed the fearful people of Earlswood spent more time in church than usual. Then a week became a fortnight and the villagers began to forget the terrible threat of the King of the Dragons. Perhaps he had gone back to his underground kingdom and quite forgotten about the tiny village that had defied him. Most people thought and hoped so.

And so the farmer's boy went back to the fields, endlessly plodding the brown furrows behind his ox-drawn plough. The carpenter became as busy as ever with his carving of benches and stools, whistling just as tunelessly as normal. The washerwoman was earning her farthings as always, encouraging her small daughters to rub and dub as hard as they could with their little red hands. As for the blacksmith, he never ceased to bellow his forge and hammer hot metal into shapes. Only the priest remained anxious and vigilant. On his knees in the church before the altar he prayed overtime for the safety and continuing happiness of all his flock.

Then one stormy night as the villagers crouched around their fires and stirred their cauldrons of rabbit stew, the roar of a dragon was heard in the wood. At the sound a feared memory returned as they glanced silently at each other. All went to bed quickly that night, their heads muffled to blot out that terrible sound. The next morning the little girl who had taunted the dragon for having no rabbits in his cap was gone. She had vanished from the earth as if she had never existed.

"The dragon is taking revenge," wept her parents. "Why didn't we fall down and worship him? Now we have lost our lovely daughter."

"We can only pray," said the sad priest. "We must believe that Our Lord in his mercy will bring her safely home."

But his words of faith were of little use to the bereaved couple.

Two nights later the dragon roared again. The following morning the farmer's son was not there at the crack of dawn to yoke his oxen to the plough. Like the girl he had disappeared without trace nor track.

It was on a Sunday evening when the dragon roared again. The priest rose from before the altar, dread in his heart. Deeply troubled he went to bed. On rising he found that his own son's bed was empty. The boy had been taken just like the others.

Over weeks and months the dragon roared again and again. More and more children were spirited away by the power the village had defied. It seemed that only the babes in arms were being spared the wrath of the dragon as the number of children in the households dwindled. Despair hung over the once cheerful community of Earlswood as the people gathered together to share their losses, and weep. Then all at once the washerwoman was pointing an accusing finger at a boy who stood alone, away from the crowd.

"And why has the carpenter's son been spared?" she cried. "Why hasn't he been spirited away by the King of the Dragons? Why is he so special?"

There were murmurs of agreement from the villagers. It did seem strange that he alone from his friends was still amongst them. There were angry mutterings that perhaps the carpenter's boy was in league with the dragon who had stolen their children. Hadn't he always been very quiet and thoughtful, this boy with golden wood-shavings in his hair? Amidst the bitterness only the priest felt a stirring of hope. For God moved in mysterious ways, and the son of the carpenter was looking very mysterious indeed. His eyes were bright as if he had seen a vision, his stance proud and assured. It was as if he was preparing for a role he was destined for. Stepping forward he addressed the blacksmith.

"Forge me a sword," he said, quietly. "And temper it hard enough to pierce the cruellest heart."

The people were astonished that such a slip of a boy could order the brawny blacksmith to do his bidding. But without a word the man went to his forge and using all his skill, crafted a weapon that the noblest of knights would be proud to bear. The boy hefted it and was satisfied. Striding across the village square he entered the church. Watched by the silent priest he knelt before the altar and praying, offered the sword for a blessing. Then he left that holy place and marched into the woods.

The villagers watched him go with hope in their hearts. It was clear to all that the carpenter's boy was setting off on a mission to resolve the heartbreak in their village. They prayed that he would be successful.

After two days trek through the gloomy woods the boy stepped out into bright sunshine. Before him curved a beaten track, rutted by the passage of many carts and horses. With no idea which way to go he glanced around and noticed an old man slumped against a milestone. Approaching he was annoyed to see that the ragged tramp was obscuring the miles to wherever on the stone. The old man paused in his munching of bread and cheese and cackled with laughter to see the boy. The boy was not amused by this familiarity.

"Pardon me, but I'd like to see what the milestone reads," he said. "If you would kindly remove yourself."

"The directions will be of no use to you," the man grinned toothlessly. He broke the bread and cheese in half and offered the boy a share. Then he reached behind the stone and produced a jug of ale. Motioning his guest to sit he watched in amusement as the boy ate and drank hungrily.

"I've been waiting for you," he chuckled. "I knew you'd be hungry after tramping for two days through the woods."

"How could you be waiting for me?" said the puzzled boy. "How could you know I was arriving?"

"One grows wise leaning against milestones," came the reply. "I've been leaning against this one since it was new. In those early days it read, 'NINETY-NINE MILES TO LONDON TOWN' but the journey might be longer or shorter now. Not that I care, for I haven't moved a mile in as many years. Not even ninety-nine paces, me being so idle."

"Then how do you earn your bread and cheese and ale?" asked the boy, sitting cross-legged beside. "Which I thank your for, old man."

"Many people pass to and fro before my milestone," was the reply. "Kings and princes and mighty churchmen have stopped to ask my advice about some worrying problem that crops up like a milestone in their own lives. In return the rich ones often throw me a plum or meat pie and a bottle of wine. Then there are the many poor and simple folk who pass by, often with weightier troubles. I advise them as best as I can and gratefully accept their gifts of bread and cheese. Over the years I've developed a keen instinct of common sense. Thus I became known as the Oracle of the Milestone, which is how I earn my living."

"But surely common sense couldn't have told you I was coming," said the boy, still perplexed. "Especially when you never leave your milestone?"

"Glance at my shoulder and tell me what you see," grinned the man.

"I see a green grasshopper on your shoulder," said the boy, gazing.

"And chirrup and chatter is all he ever does," the Oracle chuckled. "He told me some time ago about the problems your village was having with the King of the Dragons. He watched as your friends were spirited away one by one. He also watched through a crack in the church door as you knelt and prayed and offered up your sword to be blessed. My little green friend told me you would be arriving from the moment you strode into the woods. But don't you think he's getting rather plump, my tiny spy? But then he loves plum pie."

"So you and your grasshopper friend can tell me where to find the Kingdom of the Dragon," said the boy, excitedly. "Being the Oracle of the

Milestone you must know that I'm on a quest to free the children of my village from the wicked dragon who is holding them prisoner."

"And you think the sword can help you do that?" said the man, smiling at some sort of secret joke. "To slay the wicked dragon? Some advice, 'don't be too quick to confuse the wicked soul with a lonely heart'."

"Just tell me where to find this dragon," cried the boy, drawing his sword. "There'll be no confusion when this point enters his heart."

At that moment the grasshopper extended his lanky leg and chirruped into the Oracle's ear. The old man nodded and turned to the boy.

"My little spy cannot say where the King of the Dragons lives," he said. "But he knows someone who can."

As if on cue a tiny jenny wren flew in to perch on the Oracle's other shoulder. A lot of cheeping and chirruping and nodding passed between the three. Then after a quick peck of bread and cheese and a sip of ale the wren flew off. The Oracle looked at the boy, his eyes twinkling. "That was the someone who knows. But she says that as you are on a quest she can only offer you a clue where to find the Kingdom of the Dragon. She said that even very small knights must suffer a bit of hardship before they reach their goal."

"I understand the jenny wren's point of view," said the boy, impatiently. "But please, old Oracle, pass on her clue and let me be on my way."

"The clue is, look for the eye of the dragon and pass through," was the mysterious reply. Then the old man began to yawn and slump even sloppier against his milestone.

"That's hardly a clue," said the desperate boy. "Didn't the jenny wren leave a spare clue just in case the first one stumped me?"

"Oh, very well," said the sleepy Oracle. "Follow the curve of this road down into the valley. Travel along the valley bottom and you'll find what you seek where the sun goes down. And my last bit of advice, never paint a dragon as black as some would paint him, and now if you don't mind it's time for my nap," and the Oracle of the Milestone fell fast asleep against his stone, a knowing smile on his wrinkled face.

The valley was deep and green and flanked each side by mountains. As the boy strode along he noticed the beauty and the bustle of life all around him. Which was puzzling. If the wicked King of the Dragons lived hereabouts, why did this valley seem such a pleasant place? Walking beside the stream that wound and gurgled towards some distant river he enjoyed the sight of leaping fishes, of droning blue dragon-flies, of pottering creatures rolling on the muddy banks before diving into the cold waters to swim themselves clean. And everywhere contented birds tip-tailed and clucked or whistled without a care in the world. Certainly these creatures were not in fear of a valley that should be plunged in gloom. For if this was the domain of the evil dragon the boy had journeyed to slay, how come such a joyous day?

The sun was setting when the boy stopped to rest. It was bliss to fling off his sweaty clothes and bathe his aching body in the stream. But all the while the clues of the Oracle filled his thoughts.

"Look for the eye of the dragon to pass through. You will find what you seek where the sun goes down."

He intended to journey on but he felt too weary. With a sigh he sank into the soft grasses beside the stream and began to drift off.

Suddenly, through half-closed eyes, he saw it. Sitting upright he stared . . .

Outlined against the orange glow of the setting sun was a rocky peak quite unlike the others. With the sun setting and casting shadows so, all its menacing features were revealed. The fringe of spiky rocks that so resembled the ruff of the dragon who had terrorised his village. He noted the overhanging boulders that looked so much like twin flaring nostrils. There was the snake of lava flow twisting down the peak that appeared exactly like the thrashing tail of an angry dragon. And set at the centre of that weather-hewn gargoyle was a cave glowing red and gold in the sun's dying light.

"The eye of the dragon," yelled the boy at the silent hills. Suddenly he was filled with e nergy as he jumped to his feet. He ignored a jenny wren who had mysteriously appeared to perch on his shoulder, to whisper in his ear. The bird clung tight as the small knight raced to the foot of the strange peak and began to climb.

Bruised and exhausted, at last he reached the top. Though it was now deep night he was able to find his bearings from the light of the moon and stars. Gazing into the face of the dragon he was disappointed. From so close to it seemed nothing more than a jumble of fallen rock, the cave at its centre simply a cave like any other. Just then the clouds passed across the moon to produce a shadow-play. All at once the interior of the cave was revealed in flickering snatches of black and white.

"Sought and found," whispered the excited jenny wren in his ear. "The eye of the dragon, now pass through."

Drawing his sword, his heart beating fast the carpenter's boy entered the cave. Gazing around he saw a shrine. A shrine to the one he had come to slay. Painted on the walls were images of the dragon wearing a golden crown. Yet in every portrait the dragon looked so lonely and sad. He appeared to be king without subjects or friends. The wondering boy instantly guessed who the artist was. It was the dragon himself who had painted his own portrait over and over again as if to prove his existence and worth.

"For where are the fierce guardians who protect a king?" mused the boy to the tiny bird clinging to his shoulder. "Why am I standing here freely, and not in chains? This Kingdom of the Dragon is a sham. So why did he boast so and spirit my friends away? Still, for that he must pay."

"Caution, carpenter's boy," warned the jenny wren, "the dragon may be alone in his make-believe kingdom, but he still has magical power."

"And I have this sword," said the grim faced boy. "So now where . . ?"

"Try there," said the bird, pointing his beak. "The darker places."

The boy explored the dimmer regions of the cave. In the gloom he stubbed his toe against a square-cut stone. It was a step, the first of a flight that spiralled downwards towards a pin-point of light below. Carefully the boy began the decent, step after cautious step. Often he would freeze as his foot dislodged rubble that plummeted down to explode on the surface far below. Still he was not challenged. This was a strange kingdom indeed.

At the bottom he found himself in an enormous cavern lit by rows of burning brands. As the cave above, this cavern was empty of life. The only object in its vastness was a huge plinth upon which squatted a statue of the King of the Dragons looking as sad and as lonely as in the paintings above. The boy walked on and finally reached the end of the cavern. There he was confronted by a massive, iron-studded door. Gripping his sword in readiness he gently applied his shoulder . . .

From inside came a sound that made his blood run cold. He could hear shrieks and loud roars and the thuds and crashing of objects being hurled about. Enraged and thirsting for battle the small knight threw his full weight against the door.

The scene that greeted him was unexpected. He stood stunned and bewildered, trying to make sense of it all. Thinking himself about to be a witness to awful things it seemed he had stumbled into the midst of a colourful festival in full-flow. What he had imagined to be the screams of pain from poor enslaved children were screams of delight as they chased and hid amongst the overturned tables and chairs and pelted each other with plum-pies and other delicious foods. As for the loud roars the boy had heard, they were but the hearty chuckling of a very happy King of the Dragons.

A king glorying in an experience he had never known before, the luxury of company and friends. The dragon sat on a golden throne wearing a silly cap. Each time he doffed it a rabbit leapt out, much to the delight of the little girl who had been the first to be spirited away from Earlswood village. She looked perfectly happy as did the other kidnapped children dancing and singing in merriment.Suddenly all festivities ceased as a young knight they recognised to be the carpenter's boy came waving his sword and spoiling their fun. They suspected he was jealous and angry because he hadn't been spirited away to this wonderful place.

"Stop!" shouted the boy. He marched to the foot of the throne, his sword pointed at the dragon king's heart. "Confess this is some magical trick, evil creature. These children may seem to be enjoying themselves, but they are obviously victims of a clever spell. In reality their hearts must be breaking and yearning for home. So, I command you to release them from their slavery or I'll run you through with this sword that has the power to root out evil."

"Remember the advice of the Oracle of the Milestone," chattered the wren into his ear. "This dragon may not be as black as he's painted. And the sword can only destroy evil, never good."

"Be quiet, little bird," snapped the boy. He addressed the dragon in ringing tones. "Now is the time for you to bow to another's will. So bow to mine or die."

All at once the merry dragon looked exactly like his portraits and statue, sad and very lonely. Then to the boy's surprise the children rushed to defend him.

"Who says we are enslaved?" cried the farmer's son. "My enslavement was in my father's fields when I had to rise at the crack of dawn to do the work of the day. I longed to play. Now I can."

"I don't feel imprisoned at all," said the daughter of the seamstress. "Here I can enjoy myself and feel free. Here in the dragon's kingdom I don't have to peer at needles and thread in a dark room. Here I look at beautiful things and never need to squint."

"Just look at our hands now," cried the washerwoman's daughters. "Once all four of them were red and raw from scrubbing and dubbing. Now they are soft enough to feel the flutterings of the wings of that little jenny wren on your shoulder."

"And I," said the son of the priest. "I once

wished to follow my father into the church. But now I know that devotion is where kindness is. And our King of the Dragons has been kindness itself from the moment we arrived in his lonely kingdom."

"But don't you see this dragon is in league with the devil?" shouted the carpenter's boy. "Didn't he enter our village and order us to fall down and worship him?"

"And we do worship him," said the black-smith's son. He pointed. "And my father made that sword judging by the superb workmanship. But what use is it in this paradise place?"

"I intend to put it to very good use," shouted the carpenter's boy. Determined to break what he believed to be the evil spell the dragon had cast over the children he lunged with all his strength at the dragon's heart. The sword so finely forged and blessed in the village church, splintered and snapped like a flimsy prop in a Passion Play. There was no triumph in the eye of the dragon. Rather an expression of hurt and sadness as he gazed at the bewildered boy. The boy in turn glanced in confusion at the wren on his shoulder.

"My advice, remember?" murmured the bird in his ear. "Good cannot destroy good, only evil.

Perhaps I might make a suggestion, me being a bit of an Oracle myself. As the King of the Dragons is obviously good and lonely and desperate for company, and as the children of Earlswood village are entitled to a break from their drudgery back home, from time to time, what say that arrangements are made to make everyone happy?"

"What arrangements?" said the dispirited carpenter's boy. "Why should I care now I've failed in my quest, and been exposed as a fool?"

"Holidays," chirruped the cheeky jenny wren. "When the children are tired of toiling around the clock for their parents, they can return to the Kingdom of the Dragon for a well-earned rest, and rounds of never-ending parties. And why not you too, carpenter's boy? For I'll wager you often get thoroughly sick of whittling stool-legs for your father without a break to ease the tedium."

Instantly the children burst into cheers to hear such a wonderful suggestion from the tiny Oracle. Even the carpenter's boy grinned. He quite liked the idea himself.

"But everyone must return home now," he said, sternly. "To relieve the anxiety in our parent's hearts. Afterwards perhaps the arrangements could be made for visiting the dragon from time to time. What do you say, dragon?"

"A delightful idea," replied the dragon, tears brimming in his eyes as he doffed his silly cap to release another scurrying rabbit. "Company is always welcome in my kingdom, and the noisier and happier the better. The idea is so perfect my tears refuse to stop."

"We'll always be thinking of you while we're slaving away at home, kingy," grinned the little girl. "Itching for our holidays to start."

"So, to home," said the carpenter's boy, briskly. He began to shepherd the children towards the iron-studded door.

"Wait," said the dragon with a wide grin. He addressed everyone. "Will we all meet again when the dragon roars in the wood?"

"We will," shouted the children. "But kingy, please show us another magic trick before we go."

"My pleasure, so goodbye until the next time," replied the happy dragon. And he opened up his huge mouth and roared. Suddenly there was a blinding flash of light and everyone was transported in a whirling, tumbling instant back to . . .

"Good morning," smiled the toothless old Oracle of the Milestone. "I hope you happy band don't intend to eat me out of bread and cheese. How many are you?"

"Everyone who was spirited away, plus me," smiled the carpenter's boy.

"And me," said the little jenny wren, perching on the old man's shoulder. "And I'd love to know how that dragon does that vanishing trick."

"He can also pull rabbits out of his cap," said the little girl. "And we're going to see our King of the Dragons again as soon as our next holidays come around. Which will mean very often as we're nearly always get fed up with home. For myself, I can't wait to hear him roaring in the woods again."

The other children agreed. There was nothing like a good holiday to refresh the body and soul after days and weeks of long boring work.

"Well, thank you for your clues and advice, old Oracle," said the carpenter's boy. "And may every traveller who passes by throw you a plum or meat pie. And now with respect and affection we say goodbye, and to you too, jenny wren."

So saying he led the tired but happy children on the long trek back through the woods to home. They hardly starved on what was a pleasant summer's day journey, for the Oracle of the Milestone had generously donated his whole hoard of food that he stored behind the mile-stone, confident that he would soon re-stock when more passers-by in worried need of advice, smiled again when he offered them his plain common sense.

Arriving back in Earlswood village the children were hugged and sobbed over by their relieved and delighted parents. Only the little girl of the rabbits received a spanking plus her hugs for being cheeky.

The carpenter's boy was naturally the hero of the village. For it was he who had made it possible for Earlswood to become a smiling place again. A place that quickly returned to the normality of earning a living through hard work. Would there never be rest from toil, sighed the weary children? Yes, there would . . .

Sooner rather than later the roar of the

dragon was heard in the woods. Holiday time for the children once again. The little girl of the rabbits was the first to be spirited away. The rest disappeared quickly after.

As the carpenter's boy whittled his stool-legs he kept his ears cocked. Some nights he went to bed disappointed. He could only think that the King of the Dragons hated him for spoiling the party that day. Perhaps the roar he yearned for would never come.

As the remaining child of his own age left in the village, he felt very lonely. Then one night, last but not least, the carpenter's boy received the call as the dragon roared in the wood. In a whirl of flashing colour and dizzying, tilting landscapes the boy was whisked away to the Kingdom of the Dragon, not brandishing a vengeful sword, but this time with a happy heart, for now he was a child again.

# MADOC
## IN SEARCH OF
## A CHOIR

Madoc was a little Welsh dragon who lived in ancient times before humans were seen in the land. He lived with his family in a cosy cave with nice neighbours and a lovely view of the green valley below. Madoc was allowed his own private nook in the cave. His family respected his need to be alone when he practised his scales. For Madoc was always singing. His ambition was to be the best singer in the whole of Wales with the help of his

best friend, a tiny brown nightingale. The bird
was the best singing teacher a young dragon
could wish for. Every day his friend flew in to
perch on Madoc's rocky window-view and
ordered him to demonstrate the skills he had
taught. Madoc, in tones as clear as crystal, sang at
the top of his voice.

"You are now ready," said the bird, proud of
his pupil. "You can now go out and achieve your
ambition."

Madoc's family was excited for him as he and
his fluttering friend set off for the high mountain
overlooking the valley. "Good luck, Madoc,"
they cried. "Make us proud of you, and
remember to gargle your throat."

On top of the mountain sat a semi-circle of
dragons. They called themselves the Welsh
Dragon Choir, but really they were only a group
of third-rate singers. Before them stood a fat
dragon who conducted their voices with the tip
of his long tail. Shyly, Madoc approached and
made his request to join their choir.

There was a problem, of course. Madoc had
always had a problem that needed to be faced
one day. While every other dragon in Wales had

been born bright red, he had been born dull grey. It wasn't his fault, but he was the dragon who suffered.

"I'm sorry Madoc," said the choir master, firmly. "But only true Welsh dragons can join our choir. A proper Welsh dragon is red all over, while you are a muddy grey colour. We have our Welsh reputation to protect. We know you are probably the best singer in Wales, but sadly the wrong colour. Why don't you climb the Black Mountains into England? The dragons there will hire anyone to sing in their bawdy taverns, no matter what colour they are."

"But I'm a *Welsh* dragon," cried Madoc. "It isn't my fault I was born grey while my brothers and sisters were born bright red. Why won't you accept me for my singing voice?"

"Here, here," said the angry nightingale. "I'm shabby brown, so what? And I'm still the best singer in the whole of red Wales, Madoc scraping in second."

"We know how beautifully you sing, Madoc," sighed the choir master. "But sadly you are the wrong colour for us. No matter how gloriously you sang you would stick out like a sore thumb on concert nights. I'm sorry, Madoc, but I can't offer you a welcome on this hillside."

"I protest," shrilled the nightingale, perched
on a rock beside. But the choir master had
turned his fat back to conduct his semi-circle of
throaty singers once more.

The family were astonished when their beloved
Madoc came home weeping. They could hardly
believe what the heartless choir-master had said
to their brother. After sobbing out his story,
Madoc slumped miserably into a corner
surrounded by his brothers and sisters who took
turns to rub his back and ease his fit of hiccups.

"How dare a fat fool treat our brother this
way," they raged. "And just listen to his sobbing,
it's quite ruining his vocal chords."

"Quite outrageous," fumed Madoc's mother.
"And all because he was born grey instead of
bright red. So, who was ever born perfect?
Madoc is still my son, red, grey, or tastelessly
puce. He is as Welsh as the leeks that grow in
the valley below. How cruel to snub a gifted
child for such a piffling trifle."

"It insults our family name," shouted father.
"This could lead to centuries of feuding against
that fat dragon's family."

"It is the sin of it that worries me," said the listening nightingale. "Bright feathers do not a singer make, witness me. The dragons of Wales are being denied their right to listen to the best singer in the land, after me, of course."

"There are other choirs in Wales," said mother. "Choirs without a colour-bar who will snap up glorious singers for their talent alone."

"I agree," said the bird. "But we must face facts. The choir will not come to our Madoc, so Madoc must go to the choirs."

"Our Madoc, a wandering minstrel? Never," roared father. "Not my son. He can stay at home and warble to us for the rest of his life. No way is our Madoc going to peddle his talent through Wales, being sneered at because he's the wrong colour."

"Anyway, Madoc is too young to wander the world alone," said mother. "He would need a wise and supporting companion who knows about life beyond our valley. A friend who would spur him on if he suffers blow after disappointing blow, as far as his career is concerned. Which rules out this family. For at the hint of Madoc's first tear we'd rush him straight home and weep our full blame. We couldn't cope with seeing

Madoc in hopeless distress."

"But I could," smiled the nightingale, bowing his beak. "Meet the wise and strong and worldly one. I'd be honoured to guide Madoc around the pitfalls that lie between him and his goal."

"Oh, mother, father, say yes," cried Madoc, rushing from his corner. "I won't mind all the hardships of floundering through the welsh swamps, and tramping through the trees and over mountains, and being sneered at for being grey. I just know there is a choir out there who will love me for my voice. I love Dad, but I couldn't bear to spend the rest of my life warbling my songs at home. I need to sing for the whole of Wales. And if all of my loved ones fear for me, I'd feel safe in the company of my friend and teacher, the little brown nightingale."

"Madoc is making an awesome decision," agreed his brothers and sisters. "He is putting his life on the line in the hope of being acclaimed the best singer in Wales. Oh, if we were so brave. Will we be content if a little bit of his fame rubs off on us? Must we have his voice constantly reminding us that we can't sing a note? But what does it matter when we love him?"

"Very well," said Madoc's parents, though worried. "It's Madoc's life. If you are prepared to take care of him little bird?"

"Madoc's life will be more precious than my own," promised the bird. "And one day I'll be flying home to bring you the news of his enormous fame.  Please trust me."

And so, after many tearful hugs Madoc left the cosy cave that had been his refuge for the whole of his young life, to set out in search of a choir. A choir who didn't care whether a singer was red or grey. A choir with music at its soul. A choir that has been searching for a Madoc to soar their songs to Heavenly heights.

With his friend the nightingale perched on his shoulder, Madoc began the long plod across a Wales that stretched in switchbacks of green hills and valleys, the songs the friends sang echoing lustily every plod of the beautiful way.

The choir was gathered in a deep lush valley. They had been singing for two full days. But they couldn't get it right. Was there something wrong with the song? Or was there something wrong with their singing? The choir master angrily tapped his baton on the oak log that was his podium, bringing their awful wailing to an end. Everyone felt awful. The sounds that issued from their throats were not the sounds they felt in their hearts.

"We'll try it one last time," snapped the choir master. "And if you ruin this one we'll all go home for tea. Ready?"

The tired choir launched into song again.

Yet there was something different in the sound this time. Rising above their chesty bellows fluted a voice that sent shivers down many backs. The voice was so perfect that the choir master snapped his baton in two and wept. The bright red dragon singers, stunned by the wonderful notes, stopped in full-flow to listen. And still the glorious voice soared on and up, singing quite alone now . . .

"No dragon in the whole of Wales can sing like that," cried the choir master. "It must be an angel come down from Heaven to show us the way."

"Oh no it's not," said a chirpy voice from a branch beside. The nightingale swayed on his perch. "You've just heard the voice of the second best singer in Wales, the first, of course, being myself. Would you like to meet the owner of the voice who will make your choir famous throughout Wales? If he deigns to sing with you, of course. For the demands on his throat are astonishing."

"Oh, please," begged the choir master. "And quickly, before a rival choir snatches him up."

Grandly the nightingale drew himself up. With a wing he gestured towards a clump of bushes. "May I present in all his talented glory, Madoc, who I'm sure is destined for great things."

And from the bushes, as rehearsed, bounded Madoc blushing pink through his grey skin because of all the nice things said about him.

"But he's grey," said the shocked choir master. Then hurriedly. "I'm sorry, but we never allow foreign singers in our choir."

"Not even if his voice is golden?" said the angry bird. "What's the matter with you Welsh choirs? Madoc may be grey, but he's just as Welsh as you. Why this silly rule that one must be bright red to sing? Why won't you give my little friend a chance? For ages he plodded through Wales, ruining his health and his feet. And I'm beak-sore with pleading for him. Admit that Madoc can sing better than the whole bunch of you dragons put together. I advise you to snap him up before I'm forced to take him into England to sing in The Dragon's Arms Tavern."

"I'm perfectly willing to sing for my supper and somewhere dry to lay my head," pleaded the weary Madoc. "And I'd do all of your odd jobs as soon as I get my strength back. Just as long as

I can sing in a real choir. Please give me a chance, choir master, for my feet and my heart are heavy from all the hoping and endless travelling." And Madoc wept more of the tears that had dogged and dampened his dream since leaving home all that time ago. His young talent seemed right at the end of its tether.

"We agree you have a Heaven-sent voice, Madoc," said the choir master. "But where would you fit in? We could put you in the middle or at the side, or perhaps at the back out of sight, but there's jealousy to consider. My choir would get very angry if a grey dragon won all the applause. Talented as you are, you will always be a foreigner singing in a land of bright red dragons who will never accept you as Welsh. So, little nightingale, I suggest that you take Madoc home, for his future in this choir is nil. Or indeed take him over the mountains into England. He'll find plenty of work singing bawdy songs there, the English being the coarse dragons they are."

"Excuses and racial rubbish," snapped the bird. "I'll only say that you and your over-trained singers will be the losers. And I hope you all turn bright green in the night. Come, Madoc . . ."

Fluttering onto his pupil's shoulder he guided

them out of the green valley to the flatlands where they could rest and consider the gloomy future.

Night came, and with it the chirping of crickets and the honking of lonely frogs and the flashing of glow-worms in love with themselves. Madoc lay slumped amongst the lush grasses, his sad eyes gazing at the stars. Then his chest began to heave as grief overcame him again.

"Madoc," sighed the bird from the bush beside. "Will you please stop hiccupping and blubbing, I'm trying to think? Practise your scales if you need something to do. And in the morning I'll have a plan, please God."

Madoc obediently wiped his eyes and began to sing his scales like a silver bell. His astonishing voice soaring higher and higher seemed to send every insect and flatland creature into a musical frenzy. The opera sung that night was magical and sweet, and did not cease 'till dawn broke. As the sun rose the nightingale, his throat hoarse from singing, flew from the bush to tug Madoc's ear.

"I've got it!" he whispered, hoarsely. "Madoc, I think I've solved our problem. Get up and see what I can see."

"What can you see?" said Madoc, scrambling to his feet.

"Strawberries," grinned the bird. "We've been singing all night in a field of wild strawberries."

"Oh good," said Madoc. "Breakfast."

"No, no," said his friend, impatiently. "The strawberries are going to aid our next career move. I promised your family I would get you into a choir, and by Heaven I will."

"And strawberries will help?" said Madoc, puzzled.

"Not only help but solve," said the bird. "Now, Madoc, I want you to roll over and over in the strawberry beds. And do it quick while the dew is still thick, that should do the trick. Come on little dragon, jump to it."

Wondering what he was doing Madoc rolled over and over in the strawberry beds until his head was dizzy.

"Stand up and let's have a look," ordered the bird. He looked pleased. "Perfect, Madoc, you are now as red as any dragon in the land. A bit patchy maybe, but who will care when you start to sing?"

"You really think I'm red enough for a choir

to love me?" asked the anxious dragon.

"You look scrumptious," smiled the bird, hopping close to sniff and stare. "In fact you're almost good enough to eat."

"And not a trace of my horrible old grey," said Madoc, happily. All at once he was his jaunty self of old as his large feet stomped the ground for action. "So what are we waiting for, teacher? Let's find a choir and slay them with my talent. And when I'm enormously famous I'll insist that you have a small whistling role in all of my concerts."

"First things first," said the wary bird. Then he hopped onto Madoc's nose and pointed the way out of the flatlands. Soon they were climbing the side of the highest mountain in Wales. At the tip squatting in rows was the genuine article, namely The Official Welsh Dragon Choir, their lungs heaving as they bellowed out their songs. Ranged around the mountain-top were their crowds of fans, clapping every heroic solo. The nightingale whispered urgently into Madoc's ear. Immediately the eager young dragon rushed forward and pushed his way into the front row of singers. In an instant his glorious voice had

joined theirs, then suddenly leading as his throat vibrated forth notes that no singer in Wales had ever attempted before. Up and up, soaring then dipping, Madoc's voice wove a spell throughout the choir and the audience. By the end he was singing alone. At the concert's end both the choir and the audience were weeping with joy. It was as if a voice from Heaven had descended amongst them. The astonished and enraptured choir

master could hardly believe his ears and luck. Who was the singer who had crashed the concert to steal the show? And would the little red dragon agree to sing for the choir for evermore, and not for any others? His voice trembling, the choir master put the question to the nightingale who was strutting about in the role of Madoc's singing agent.

"I think my client will agree to sing in your choir," he said. Then hurriedly. "But Madoc never sings in the rain. That must be in his contract."

That might be difficult," said the choir master. "For it's always raining in Wales."

No sooner had he said the words when the rain began to bucket down on the mountain-top.

The audience quickly scattered to shelter in their cosy caves. And cruelly and mercilessly the torrent began to wash away Madoc's new identity. Strawberry coloured puddles began to form around Madoc's feet until he was finally exposed in all his greyness. The nightingale sighed the sigh he had sighed over such a long time. Once again the game was up. He cocked a tired eye at the choir master, knowing what was to come. The red face of the pompous conductor was glowing even redder, with anger.

"Don't tell us," said the sad bird. "Madoc is the best singer you've ever heard, but he's the wrong colour."

"Too right he is," yelled the choir master. "You've got five minutes to leave our mountain. We want no foreign grey dragons slipping into our choir."

"But I'm a genuine Welsh dragon," cried Madoc, despairingly. "It's only because of a freak of nature that I was born grey."

But his appeal fell on deaf ears. The Welsh Dragon Choir were anxious to see the back of the wonderful singer who made them sound off-key, and further mocked their pride by being drearily grey.

So Madoc and his staunch friend were back on the road again. Once their wanderings had been hours, then days and weeks, now their quest was drifting into years. And never once did even the humblest choir give Madoc a chance. Not a single choir would overlook his greyness. The pair became legendary throughout Wales as they tramped through the villages singing their beautiful songs. But it was Madoc's greyness that caused most gossip, never the quality of his glorious voice.

Then one day from sheer weariness, Madoc collapsed.

The concerned bird fluttered to gaze into his friend's eyes. Sadness gazed into approaching death. They were in a glade from which snaked three paths. One path led to home, the second led over the mountains into England, while the third led to a peace that would ease all the poor dragon's suffering.

"I cannot go on, precious nightingale," whispered Madoc. "I am weary and need to rest. I feel a desperate need to crawl along that path that offers peace from all my problems. Please don't stop me, little friend. And don't accompany me this time, I know the way. Yours will be the path to my youthful home. Go bearing good tidings and all of my love."

And leaving the nightingale weeping on a fallen bough the young dragon, aged so much beyond his years, plodded down the path that would grant him peace. And the path was suddenly filled with glorious light. Then the humble little bird saw a host of angels descending from the sky to take Madoc in their arms, to bear him upwards singing. And the voice raised above all was Madoc's, glorious and true, fading away as he entered into a new and happy world. Madoc had passed into the place he belonged.

Drying his tears the little nightingale set off along another path. After two days of persistent flying he reached his goal. Breathing heavily he perched on the sill of the private nook where his pupil had practised his musical skills. The family came rushing.

"What news, little bird?" they asked excitedly. "Is Madoc as famous as we all knew he would be?"

"Madoc's singing fame has soared into the realms of Heaven," said the little bird, choking back a sob.

"And will he be coming home to sing for us again?" they asked. "For this is where it all started."

"Madoc now sings in the greatest choir on earth or in Heaven," said the bird, openly weeping. "And he will sing to each one of us when we need his presence close."

"To think, our Madoc, a freaky grey dragon, is so applauded," said mother, wonderingly. "And so famous that I can't reach out and touch him."

"But we'll always feel his presence," said father. "He is in this nook and everywhere we turn."

"And in our dreams when we go to sleep," said the children.

And Madoc was.

# SNIFFY'S
## STORY

S niffy the dragon yearned for a job in life.
He wanted to be useful and make his family
proud of him.

"I'd love to be a keep-fit teacher," he said,
sneezing all over his loving brothers and sisters.
"If only I didn't wheeze when I did knee-bends."

His brothers and sisters all had good jobs.
However, they hadn't been born with their poor
brother's handicap. Sniffy was constantly catching
olds. Though he was bright and cheerful, the

moment he started to say something interesting his chest would begin to wheeze and his nose to run. The worst times were when his weekly colds combined to become full-blown monthly 'flu. His family despaired as they mopped his red, watering eyes, for they loved him dearly. How they wished they could find a cure for him. They had tried most remedies. They found that making him chew raw bitter lemons brought him relief, but only for a short time. It was a suggestion from Sniffy's youngest sister that changed his life.

"What if one morning we got Sniffy up very early to do some keep-fit stretches and knee-bends?" she said. "Then while he's looking fit we can force five bitter lemons down his throat to keep the colds at bay. Then, while he's blowing his nose as hard as possible we could rush him down to the Dragon Job Centre. With his cold on hold he would easily impress the officials with his fitness and secure the job he desires. Then with a career safely under his belt we could rush him back home to snuffle and sniffle and sneeze to his hearts content."

"Sniffy would be on a trial period if he got the keep-fit job," said his worried mother. "He would need sacks of bitter lemons to get through that."

"It's the landing of the job that's important," explained one of Sniffy's brothers. "Then if his employer complains about Sniffy's delicate health we'll get a sharp lawyer to sue for unfair dismissal."

"Dragging Sniffy through the law courts would play havoc with his chest," said father, shaking his head. "I think Sniffy should go to the Job Centre as he is. He might strike lucky with an employer who suffers from colds himself."

"But not cold upon cold upon 'flu, and back again," said the young sister. "Even employers eventually recover, while Sniffy never does. I think my idea is the best. Let's concentrate on getting Sniffy a job. We can tackle the arising problems later."

"Well if that's what you think," said her doubtful father. "But will our Sniffy bear up under the strain of it all?"

"I'll bear the strain, dad," vowed Sniffy, violently blowing his nose. "And when I've risen to become the top keep-fit expert in the dragon world I'll buy you and Mum a posher cave."

"Just don't bring your hankies home when

you're successful," smiled mother. "Your nose always causes me problems on washing day."

And so the family was agreed. All Sniffy needed was to be freed from the straight-jacket of illness to make his mark on the world.

Early the next morning, stuffed to choking with bitter lemons and blowing his nose like a fog-horn, Sniffy was rushed to the Dragon Job Centre. The official regretted that he didn't have a vacancy for a keep-fit teacher, but still she did have an empty position in the Royal Security Guard. Sniffy looked disappointed until his family assured him that it sounded like a very important job. They advised him to snap it up. Hardly sniffing at all thanks to all the lemons, Sniffy agreed to the terms of the trial period.

"By the way," said the official, concerned. "Is your eyesight alright, because your eyes seem to water a lot? One needs perfect eye sight to be a Royal Security Guard."

What you see are tears of happiness," said his sister, quickly. "Sniffy is a very emotional young dragon."

"Very well," said the brisk official. "Report here at first light and you'll be assigned to your first post."

Sniffy and his family were overjoyed as they lumbered back up the hill to home. At last all the children had jobs. It was a huge worry lifted from their shoulders.

That night all Sniffy could talk about was the job he was starting in the morning. His happiness was such that he spent most of the evening marching up and down the cave looking every inch the smart security guard. And his family applauded him, for they loved their Sniffy dearly. Then suddenly his sinuses went haywire. All at once he began to cough and wheeze. It was an ominous sign. It was clear that the four colds Sniffy had suffered in a row were turning into 'flu. He was quickly rushed to bed and covered with warming straw. Then he was force-fed one half-dozen bitter lemons and ordered to rest.

"Will I be well enough to start my new job in the morning?" he snuffled. "Only I want you all to be proud of me."

"With plenty of sleep you'll be as fit as a flea in the morning," comforted his sister.

"I don't like Sniffy having to report for work like this," grieved mother. "Are you sure we can't go with him?"

"Sniffy must face his challenge alone," said a brother. "Mothers aren't allowed in the work-space when sons report for work."

"Just look, bless him," said the young sister, gazing tenderly at the huge pile of steaming straw. "He's fast asleep now. And I'll bet his dreams are filled with hopes for tomorrow, and the start of his career."

"I think someone should remove that straw," said his father, worried. "Sniffy's nose is sparking and we don't want him to burst into flames on the eve of his working life."

But there was no need for worry. At the crack of dawn Sniffy was up and as fit as the family had ever seen him. There was no sign of the 'flu that had laid him low the previous evening, probably due to his state of excitement. After a quick snack of bitter lemons he fairly raced down the hill to the Dragon Job Centre, cheerfully waving his anxious family goodbye.

"You can breathe fire, I take it?" said the lady dragon official, blowing her nose. "Because that is essential to the job."

Sniffy happily puffed a few sparks. Seeing the lady frown he tried again, bravely battling the wheezes that rose from his chest. This time he produced a weak tongue of flame.

"Well it is very early in the morning," said the lady, grudgingly. She blew her nose again.

"Have you got a cold?" said Sniffy, interested. "You should try raw bitter lemons, they do wonders for me."

"My cold is my own business," said the official, coldly. "I ask the questions here. So, are you ready to take up the post of Royal Security Guard for a trial period?"

"I am," said Sniffy, happily. "And will I be promoted if I do well?"

"If you don't do well you'll be sacked," snapped the lady. "Now listen carefully, you are to report to Sombre Castle to guard a rich and beautiful princess against the hordes of gold-diggers who are trying to win her hand. Your job will be to see them off in no uncertain manner. You don't object to violence, I hope?"

"My mum says I've got a wicked little temper when I'm roused," said Sniffy, proudly. "She says nobody flies off the handle as quickly as me."

"Good," was the reply. Then she tapped her desk with a red-painted claw and eyed Sniffy sternly. "But there is one suitor you will allow to cross the drawbridge of the castle. He is the handsome Prince Charming who the King approves of. You'll recognise him by the peacock feather in his cap. He also has extremely shapely legs and a brilliant white smile. Have you got that?"

"Got it," said Sniffy. He rose and shouldered his sack of lemons. "And can you tell me the way to Sombre Castle?"

"Do you see the mountain with the top lost in the clouds?" said the lady, pointing a manicured claw. "Well, the castle is somewhere in the mist."

"Thank you miss," said Sniffy, eager to be off. But his natural kindness caused him to turn back. "Would you like one of my bitter lemons for your cold?"

"What cold?" said the lady, irritably. "It's just a sniffle."

"You might think it's a sniffle, but you've a full-blown cold coming on," said Sniffy. "I'm an expert on colds and I know what I'm talking about."

"And I'm an expert on jobs," flared the lady official. "So I advise you to get about yours. Unless you want to lose it before you've got it."

Sniffy had barely hurried from her office

before she began to wheeze and sneeze. Oh no, she prayed, she hoped she wasn't coming down with a cold . . .

How Sniffy managed to climb all the way up the mountain to Sombre Castle he never knew.

He was forced to stop quite a few times to chew a lemon, to ease the tightness in his chest. But this first job meant everything to him. He was determined not to let his loving family down. After a lot of nose-blowing he reached his goal.

As he lumbered and panted onto the drawbridge of Sombre Castle he spied a pauper Prince strumming a lute and singing a silly love song under a window. Obviously he was trying to lure away the rich and beautiful Princess who was leaning from the window and batting her eye lashes at the scoundrel.

From the next-door window the King was bellowing at the suitor to get back to his pig-pen in Wales and to stop singing rubbish in a foreign language.

"And about time too," yelled the King when he saw Sniffy scrambling to the rescue. "What do you think I employ dragons for?"

# Sniffy's Story

It took only a short blast of sparks from Sniffy's nose to discourage the penniless Prince of Wales. Throwing away his lute the young man was soon haring back to the Black Hills and his mud-pie castle. The Princess withdrew her long mane of blonde hair from the window and sullenly slammed it shut. Once more she had been foiled in her plan to run away with romance.

This first success to his credit, Sniffy, with the help of his sack of lemons to ease his symptoms, settled into the job he hoped would earn him promotion and afford his parents a classier cave for their old age. Through the following days he chased off a few more stony-broke princes who fancied their chances with the beautiful Princess. Then unfortunately his supply of lemons ran out. It was just his luck that he was in the middle of a wheezing and sneezing fit when a ragged vagabond came striding across the drawbridge to try to capture the heart of the Princess with his wild gypsy dances. The Princess was enraptured. Tying her long blonde hair to the frame of the window she swarmed down the tresses, snipping herself free in a crew-cut style as she reached the ground. Then, under the watering eyes of Security Guard Sniffy, the pair ran away to be as poor as possible but in love forever. There was worse to come . . .

A few minutes later a young man with shapely calves and a gleaming smile came mincing across the drawbridge. Rubbing his smarting eyes Sniffy noticed that the youth was wearing a peacock's feather in his cap. It was Prince Charming come to claim his bride. At this point the heart of the small dragon sank into the soles of his feet. He know what was coming.

"Welcome, noble Prince," called the King from his window. "My beautiful daughter awaits your flattery and marriage proposal in the next window."

"I fear not, your Majesty," replied the Prince, his perfect smile fading. "All I can see is an empty window with long blonde tresses hanging down and streaming in the breeze."

"Gone, my beautiful daughter gone?" cried the King. "Please God she hasn't run off with the lad who polishes my spoons. I've noticed the secret smiles that pass between them. Now I'll be the butt of sniggers and spoon jokes amongst my courtiers. Heaven preserve me in my grief. Now what do I do?"

"I suggest you look to your security, Sire," said the bitter Prince Charming. "That is where the blame lies," and he flounced away on his shapely legs to chat up another Princess.

Quite rightly the anger of the King focused on Sniffy who had found a shrivelled lemon in the corner of his sack and was chewing it down as fast as possible.

"Well, you blunderer!" bellowed the King. "You were supposed to be watching over my flighty daughter. Did you see nothing?"

"I'm sorry, your Majesty," said Sniffy, humbly. "But my eyes were watering at the time. Though I did see a blurred image of a raggle-taggle gypsy lad holding hands with a beautiful bald maiden as they ran by."

But Sniffy knew he was wasting his words with excuses. He knew he was about to lose his first job. With lowered nose and eyes he listened as the raging King ordered him off the draw-bridge, and to report back to the Dragon Job Centre.

"Tell them you're useless," bawled the King after him. "Tell them because of your unfitness for the job I've lost a daughter to a tinkering saucepan mender. Tell them that!"

Back at the Dragon Job Centre Sniffy didn't quote a word of the angry King. He simply said to the very ill lady dragon behind the desk that he and the King had decided to part, rather than to stay together.

"In other words you've been sacked," croaked the lady dragon, mopping at her large nose. "And I'm not surprised. I suppose you are here to beg for another job as if they grow on trees?"

"Yes please," said Sniffy. "I'll even take a job nobody else wants. I just need to be successful and make my family proud of me. My dream is to earn enough wages to buy my parents a smart cave in a nice area."

"Well, I just happen to have the perfect job for you," said the lady, dabbing at her watering eyes. "You've heard of St George, I take it? We all know how conceited he is, always looking for ways to be even more popular. Well, he has applied to this office for a dragon to die in a good cause. He needs a dragon whocan bind a pretty maiden to a stake and demand a huge ransom for her safe return. Then while the dragon . . . that's you . . . is roaring and spitting fire, St George will thunder down on his horse and spit you through the heart with his lance. Do you want the job, for nobody else does? You'll be paid treble wages, of course. Or rather your family will, you being stone-dead. That is the job, take it or leave it."

"I'll take it," said Sniffy, bravely. "At least I'll die in full employment. Thank you very much, Miss. And may I say that your cold is getting no better. May I suggest raw bitter lemons? Going by your symptoms, am I right in saying that this is your third cold in a row? I suppose you know that a fourth cold will herald the arrival of full blown 'flu?"

"I'll worry about my colds," said the lady dragon, coldly. "You should be worrying about your remaining day of life. Report to the Field of Battle first thing in the morning. The arrangements have been made . . ."

St George had organised everything down to the last detail. The pretty maiden was already tied to the stake, practising her squeals just as Sniffy turned up for work. He was pleased to discover he was a natural actor. His angry roars and fire-breathing were very realistic. But his fears were much more real. He did wonder throughout rehearsals why he should die just because he needed to work so badly. But he had accepted the job and he was determined to do the best he could, his family being on treble wages when they come to claim his body.

The hills around were packed with people who had come to see their hero St George slay the wicked dragon. Then they all fell silent as their champion thundered down on Sniffy who was standing before the maiden at the stake, frantically realising that he had forgotten to bring a supply of lemons. His nose was weeping like a tap and his chest was coughing out billions of germs as St George levelled his lance to stab him through the heart. Then Sniffy sneezed. It was an extraordinary sneeze. It had the strength of a gale. Such a sneeze could only have one result. It blew St George clean from his horse. There was a great roar of anger from the crowd who had come to see Sniffy spitted. There was a deep groan of sadness as St George was carried from the field on his shield, already sniffling and snuffling in the grip of a heavy cold. Seeing the vengeful mood of the crowd, Sniffy took to his large flat heels and fled, not stopping until he found refuge in a thick wood. For a long time he wept for the failure his life had become. He

grieved to have let his family down so badly.
Now they would never receive his treble wages,
for he was still alive. The young dragon no
longer wished to live.

Sobbing quietly he blew his nose on a soft
patch of moss and went to sleep. Softly rustling
the leaves fell from the trees to cover him. For
years and then centuries they continued to fall on
the hibernating dragon, hiding his bulk from the
prying eyes and the hatred of those who feared
and would kill dragons.

And Sniffy slept and slept until . . .

"Until I came through the woods and kicked you on the nose," grinned George. "I'm glad about that. If I hadn't you would have dreamed on for another thousand years, and I would never have made such a good friend so full of wonderful stories. My dread now is that the doctor will come in the morning and pronounce us completely well. For we do feel completely fit now, don't we, Sniffy?"

"Never felt better, little George," said Sniffy, sadly. "And we know what it means, don't we? Our wonderful times together are about to end."

"All because of a modern doctor's clever medicine," said George, brushing away a tear. "For me it's back to school to study as hard as I can to become a writer. And you, Sniffy, what will you do? Please don't burrow back under the leaves in the wood and grieve more hundreds of years away."

"No, my kindly St George," said Sniffy. "After the doctor's wonderful treatment I feel fitter than I have ever felt in my life. In fact I feel so fit that my magical powers are returning. I intend to transport myself back to my beginnings, back to the humble cave of my loving family. There I will start my life all over again and achieve the ambitions my sickliness barred me from."

"So," said George, weeping openly now. "That means I will never see you again. You'll fade just like a memory."

"No I won't, my precious," said the dragon, tenderly patting the boy. "When I'm gone visit the library and borrow the biggest and thickest and most colourful dragon book they have. Leaf through it and you'll see me. Look for the fiercest dragon in the book. He will be bright blue and orange and healthily breathing fire at all types of knights and princes and so-called Saints. Then look closely into the eyes of that proud dragon, my little George. For there you will see a broad wink.  That wink will be for you, sending my love across the centuries . . ."

Then suddenly there was no time left to speak. There was knock on George's bedroom door. In an instant Sniffy was a white mouse again, curled up inside the budgie cage.

"Feeling better, are we," smiled the doctor, checking George's chest with his cold stethoscope, mother hovering behind. "We certainly sound it. In my opinion, fit as a fiddle to go back to school."

"Would you check Sniffy, doctor?" said George, anxiously. "Only he has to go on a very long journey into his past, and he needs to be fully fit for it."

The amused doctor put the stethoscope through the bars of the budgie cage and listened gravely. Winking at George's mother he turned to the boy, his face doctor-solemn. "This mouse in a budgie cage who could well be a dragon is now super-fit. The treatment you shared has done the trick for both of you."

"It will be the Lemsip," said George. "Sniffy always swore by lemons for curing colds."

"And the antibiotic tablets, George," said his mother, blushing. "The doctor knew what he was doing."

"He'll be alright now," said the doctor as mother showed him to the door. "Just make sure he wraps up warm."

"I'm so relieved," said his mother. "There were nights when he sounded quite delirious. Sometimes it seemed he was talking to someone who wasn't there."

"We all talk to someone when alone, even dragons," said the doctor. He smiled wistfully.

"Especially the young ones who live through

imagination. What a pity they have to become grown-ups like us, worrying about bills and becoming more and more cynical. Oh well, goodbye," he added.

That afternoon George put on his anorak and scarf and sadly carried the budgie cage with Sniffy inside, into the wood. Into the pile of disturbed leaves he set free the small white mouse.

Suddenly the piles of leaves erupted as Sniffy transformed from a mouse into the tallest, most beautiful blue and orange dragon it was possible to imagine.

From his huge jaws jetted a white-hot flame of fire. Then the fire subsided.

"Goodbye, my little St George," he said gently. "And don't forget when you leaf through your dragon books, I'll be the one with the wink. Don't forget to wink right back, for that will be the signal of love across the ages. I'll never, never forget you, my George, please don't forget me. Remember the stories I told you. Write them down one day in memory of me. And now it's time, the centuries are calling me back. Goodbye . . . goodbye . . ."

And waving and calling, his eyes streaming tears, George watched his best friend vanish in a blaze of white light. And there was nothing left but a heap of smouldering leaves.

His eyes still weepy and dazzled, George stumbled back home and sobbingly flung his arms around his mother. Though she couldn't understand his distress, she held him close for a long time.

Alone in his bedroom, George leafed through his exercise book. All the stories were there. He began to read them. Sadly at first, he began to smile, then chuckle. In no time at all he was back in the world of the dragons. Rising, he crossed to the window. The moon was full. He peered. Was that a dragon passing across its face, or just a strangely-shaped cloud? Who knew? Who would ever know?